love in the countdown

lily anh nam

LOVE IN THE COUNTDOWN

Copyright © 2025 by Lily Anh Nam.

Cover design by Mayumi

Typography by Occult Goddess

Edited by Deliciously Dark Editing

ISBN: 978-1-967610-01-3 (paperback), 978-1-967610-00-6 (e-book)

First Edition: May 2025

love in the countdown

When heartbreak leaves Emily homeless on New Year's Eve, her world shatters—but in the ruins of a failed relationship lies the spark of a new beginning

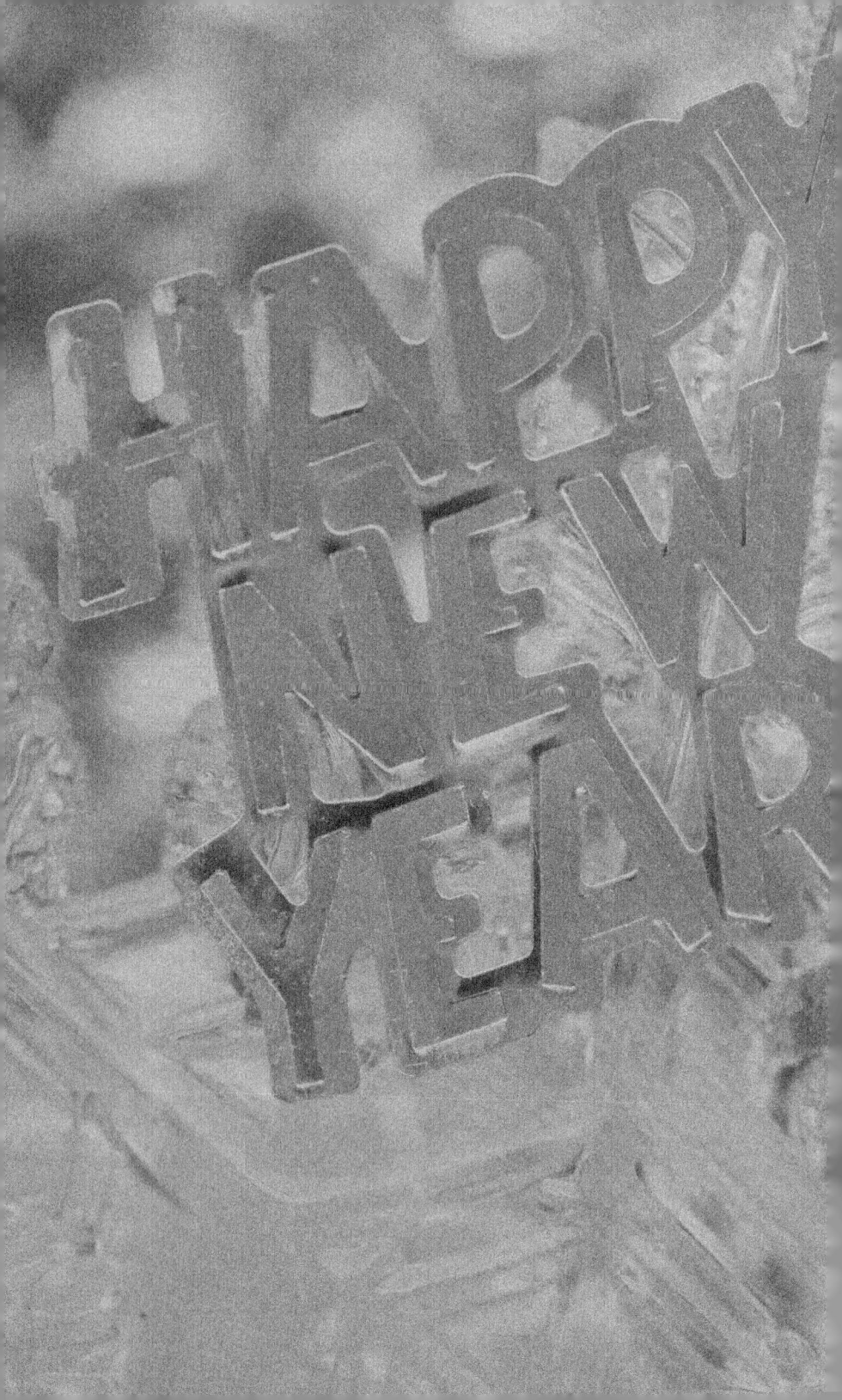

Love in the Countdown

Lily Anh Nam

This book is dedicated to my beautiful family.
Without you, I am lost.
I love you all with everything that I am.

I also dedicate this book to anyone who has a story
to tell and is looking for that push to write their book.
This is your sign. Write your book.
Your story deserves to be told.

content warning

This book is a contemporary romance for 18+ readers only. This is not intended to be a comprehensive list of the contents. Please read responsibly and mind your triggers.

Love in the Countdown contains sexually explicit scenes, mental health issues (including depression), non-life threatening pregnancy complications, pregnancy disability, post-partum depression. It also contains brief mention of toxic parents.

smut guide

For those looking for a good time. Or for those who wish to avoid it. You will find sexually explicit content in the following chapters:

contents

1
Emily

I woke up this morning without a clue it would end with me being single and homeless before the day was over. The thought of Logan breaking up with me seemed absurd a month ago. In fact, it was almost laughable. I thought we were happy and in love. I was so confident in us.

The weight of Logan's unhappiness, recounted over three years of our relationship, hit me hard; each word was a heavy stone in my gut.

Despite the racing thoughts in my head, I try to keep my composure. His words are sharp and cold. Callous. They slice through me as a stark contrast to the future I envisioned with him. I'm desperately trying to understand them. To wrap my mind around how disconnected we were in our relationship.

Logan's droning voice fills the room; the repetitive phrase, "no future," echoes in my ears, each repetition a fresh stab of pain. He ends his hurtful speech with a surprising announcement. He wants me to move out as soon as possible. My throat constricts, a silent scream trapped behind the lump of panic rising in my throat.

The worst part? It's New Year's Eve, and we had plans tonight. His graciousness in breaking up with me before noon meant I had the entire afternoon to make new plans with my friends. The urge to slap him was so strong I had to sit on my hands. It was probably illegal to hit a police officer, no matter how heartless they may be.

I didn't need to add jail time to the growing list of issues in my life right now. Or, well, ever.

The sheer thoughtlessness of waiting until New Year's Eve, a day brimming with hope and expectation, to end things feels like a cruel twist of fate, a stark contrast to the celebratory atmosphere surrounding it. Not to mention the fact that Logan knows how superstitious I am about New Year's Eve. I always take extra care to make sure nothing bad happens on this one day. I don't want to have a whole year of bad luck ahead of me.

Asshole.

The same thought keeps repeating itself in my mind as he drones on and on... How did I not see this coming?

Sure, our relationship was easygoing. We rarely ever fought or disagreed about many things. We share the same hobbies and work ethics. And the sex? Well, that was fine, too, I suppose. So, where did things go wrong?

I try to run through the events of this morning to figure out if there was a tipping point or even any clue that this was where the day was going to lead us, but I'm still baffled.

It's been just like any other typical day for us both. We woke up in the same bed together and went to our respective gyms with plans to have breakfast when we both got home. We normally go to the same gym where we first met. However, I also split my time at a popular yoga studio in town. So, today was my yoga day.

The only unusual occurrence was Logan did not answer the phone when I called him to let him know I was done and heading back to our apartment.

Honestly, when I walked into our apartment and he told me he wanted to talk to me, my heart leaped to my throat at the prospect of him finally proposing. I mean, after three years together and discussing our future many times, it would be a natural assumption.

Boy, was I wrong.

Logan had taken me by the hand and led me into our living room. He sat me down on the couch, where I perched expectantly, thinking this was it. The moment we had been talking about. I tried to school my features into a mask of nonchalance, though my knee bounced restlessly.

Only, instead of getting on one knee, he'd sat across from me and told me the complete opposite.

It took a few seconds for my mind to register what was happening. Once the news settled in, I sat there in quiet disbelief while he disassembled our last three years together like it meant absolutely nothing to him, as if we didn't live together and share most of our free time together, as if we didn't share mutual friends or go to the same gym.

But, not to worry; since it was not yet noon, I had plenty of time to make plans with my friends since I was clearly no longer invited to go out with his friends anymore.

Did I really want to make last-minute plans for New Year's Eve? I know that all my friends have had their plans set for weeks, if not a couple of months. I would feel so awkward trying to join in on their fun while moping about my newfound single-woman status.

Regardless, how could Logan do this to me? Do this to us?

After what feels like an hour, Logan finally gives me a sympathetic look as he nervously takes my hand and apologizes to me like we're strangers. Then he takes off to shower while I sit speechless on our couch.

Now what?

♥ ♥ ♥ ♥ ♥

3

I never thought I would be alone on New Year's Eve, crying my little heart out while watching episodes of Friends on Netflix, yet here I am. I've been running through the conversation with Logan from this morning over and over. I still haven't figured out how I missed the signs that he'd been unhappy.

From what I vaguely remember during his speech this morning, he had been unhappy for a while. At least a few months. But where were the signs?

I feel so blindsided.

Betrayed.

While I sit here having a pity party, he's out with his work buddies. I didn't end up reaching out to any of my friends to tag along with their plans; I didn't want to be the black cloud and bring down the mood with news of my breakup.

Plus, I'm not ready or in the mood to tell everyone about our breakup.

So, here I am.

Alone.

On New Year's Eve.

Crying while eating my favorite mint chocolate chip ice cream and drinking from the bottle of my favorite pinot noir, surrounded by piles of tissues as if they could shield me from reality.

I figured I could give myself at least one night to feel sorry for myself before I picked up the pieces of my life and moved on.

But tonight, I would allow myself to feel my heart as it broke into a million pieces.

Reluctantly, I flip the channel to tune into the live show of Times Square. The crowd looks on with hope and excitement as they wait for the ball to drop. I've always loved this part. The countdown until the ball drops has always brought me so much joy. Usually, Logan would be right there with me to share a toast and a sweet kiss as the clock struck midnight, signaling the end of another year and the beginning of a new one.

But tonight, I'm alone, and instead of champagne, it's wine.

The crowd at Times Square becomes boisterous as the clock shows the last minute before midnight. Their bright smiles and exuberant mood did nothing to lift her spirits. If anything, the joyous atmosphere made the weight of her predicament feel heavier, like a weighted blanket.

I grab a fresh tissue and wipe my tears away. Blowing my nose and balling the tissue up to throw at the TV. It's the best I can do, given the circumstances.

The camera pans around the crowd and returns to the giant ball, which is now the focus of everyone's attention. Finally, the moment everyone has been waiting for arrives. The ten-second countdown. The noise escalates as the crowd joins in exuberantly counting down the seconds.

10…

9…

8…

7…

6…

5…

4…

3…

2…

1!

I raise my glass of wine in a mock toast and take a generous sip.

"Happy New Year," I murmur.

In the morning, I will deal with the aftermath of what the ending of this relationship entails.

Like moving out.

Fuck. Me.

2
Emily

I woke up bleary-eyed and hungover on New Year's Day, though not because I had too many glasses of champagne to ring in the new year, but because I ended up finishing the entire bottle of wine by myself.

No regrets, though.

Okay, maybe some regrets, judging by the pounding in my head.

Groaning, I roll over in bed and cover my face with my hands to block out some of the harsh sunlight streaming in from the bedroom windows. Spike meows in protest when I dislodge him from his perch on my belly, where he usually likes to sleep most nights. I look over to Logan's side of the bed to find it empty. I know he came home last night after I finally crawled into bed, but he isn't anywhere in sight at the moment.

Logan is as straight-laced as they can get. He rarely drinks or breaks the rules. As a cop, he follows the law to the letter. I bet he's probably already eating his stupid Paleo breakfast and texting his buddies to get together at our gym for a New Year's Day workout.

Ugh.

Normally, I would be on board with going with him to our gym, but I doubt he would want me to tag along, given our circumstances.

Fuck.

Breaking up doesn't just mean moving out, but now I'll have to find a new gym to join or risk him thinking I let myself go because we broke up. A problem for another day, but not today.

I slowly get myself out of bed and wash up in the bathroom. It takes me longer than normal to complete my routine, the pounding headache making my movements feel sluggish. The sounds from downstairs finally prompt me to go to the kitchen. Steeling myself for the inevitable, I drag my steps as I dread how today will go.

The smell of bacon and eggs assaults my senses. My stomach gurgles, and I can't tell if it's because of hunger or in revolt. My heart hammers against my ribs in anticipation of the impending encounter.

I come to a stop when I find Logan in the breakfast nook where we usually start our days together. Normally, seeing him—his warm smile and the comforting scent of his cologne—brings me peace, but today, I feel nothing but indifference. He's eating his breakfast and reading the news on his cell phone.

"Um… hi," I say stiffly. My voice comes out in a harsh croak.

Startled, Logan looks up from his phone. Apparently, I wasn't making enough noise with my slow creep down the stairs.

"Oh. Hi," he responds. He frowns as if he's uncomfortable with the situation. "I made breakfast if you want any…"

"Thanks…" *Wow, this is so much more awkward than I thought it would be.*

I make myself a plate and then become paralyzed with indecision about where I should even sit. Do I sit with him and pretend everything is normal and be friendly? Do I move into the living room and eat by myself? Unsure what to do, I stand there for a few moments until Logan clears his throat and gets up from the breakfast table. He grabs his plate and makes his way into the kitchen. As he walks toward me, I try to move out of the way, but since our apartment is small, there isn't a lot of space to move around each other. After some awkward maneuvering, I make my way to the breakfast nook with my plate of food.

I'm slowly working through the scrambled eggs when he clears his throat again and turns to me. Pausing with my fork halfway to my mouth, I glance up at Logan.

"So… umm… do you think you can have your things moved out today?"

I nearly drop my fork as my jaw drops open, food still in my mouth.

Is he serious?

"Are you serious?"

"Well… yeah, I mean. We broke up so…"

I waited, a silence stretching between us, for him to elaborate, but apparently, that was all he had to say about the matter.

"You mean, we broke up not even twenty-four hours ago, and you want me to move out… today?"

"Um… yeah, I guess so." He rubs the back of his neck and grimaces.

I stare at him, my gaze unwavering, trying to comprehend the situation. The tension in the air is palpable.

"Logan. I don't have a place to go." *Because we have been living together the entire time we've been together.*

"Well, can't you move back into your parents' place or something?"

Now I'm getting pissed. He knows that even though my parents still live in their home a few towns over, we have not been on friendly terms. I haven't seen or talked to my parents in well over a decade at this point. Even before Logan and I got together. So, no, moving in with my parents is not a fucking option.

"I am not moving in with my parents," I finally say to him, my voice firm despite my inner turmoil.

"But babe... I mean, Emily, you can't... stay here," he stammers, shoulders hunched.

I thought I was angry before, but now I'm furious. Did he really expect me to be moved out less than twenty-four hours after breaking up with me? This makes me wonder... How long has he been planning on breaking up with me if he could so callously suggest moving in with my parents as if it's even a reasonable option?

Trying to swallow down my impulse to strangle him with my bare hands, I take a deep breath and look him in the eyes.

"I am not moving in with my parents." Inhaling another breath to calm myself before I continue. "I need time to find a new place and figure things out."

He shifts on his feet, looking so uncomfortable that I almost feel bad for him until I remember why we're in this situation. I imagine impenetrable walls of stone growing around my heart, each brick representing a fresh wound, sealing off the possibility of more.

"Okay, but I want you to leave here as soon as possible."

The words were devoid of warmth or inflection; Logan's monotone command echoed through the emptiness of the room. Any tenderness I had for him is gone. My eyes brimming with unshed tears, I nod slowly, then look away, unable to meet his gaze any longer. I refuse to let him see me cry. I have nothing else to say to him at this moment. No matter what happened, it would change nothing; the damage was done. There was no turning back for us now that my walls were up.

A few more agonizing moments of silence hung heavy in the air, the only sound the quiet hum of the refrigerator before he slunk away, leaving me alone with my cold meal and a heavy sense of foreboding. I wonder absently if Logan had secretly hoped I would grovel or beg for him to let me stay. Or if he had expected a different reaction, but the words "I don't love you anymore" hung heavy and final in the air; the silence that followed felt like a physical weight, crushing any hope of reconciliation.

So much for a good start to the new year.

This year is going to suck.

3
Emily

I'm lying on the couch with Spike while his sister, Buffy, warms my feet as I search for apartments on my phone. I've been at it for what feels like hours, but in reality, it probably hasn't been that long. My search has come up with nothing affordable in any of the nicer areas of town. The ones I found that fit my budget are probably unsafe for a single woman to live alone.

With a groan of frustration, I tossed my phone onto the couch, buried my face into a pillow, and let out a muffled scream. My wild flailing sent Spike tumbling, eliciting a furious, outraged meow. He flicks his tail at me in agitation as he saunters away.

Logan is gone for the day. He normally would tell me where he's headed, but since we're at a standoff, he left without a single word to me. Judging by his outfit, he was likely going to the gym to get in a workout. Something we would have normally done together, but since I'm still nursing a hangover, I had no desire to get off the couch anytime soon.

I still can't believe he expected me to have my bags packed so soon after dropping a bomb on my life.

I met Logan three years ago when I joined the local gym,

which was around the same time I started my first nursing job at the nearby hospital. I was never an athlete in school, nor was I ever very active, but I felt it was necessary to start a fitness routine to help me get healthy after ruining my diet and waistline with endless hours of studying and eating trash during nursing school. The stress and the calories have not been kind to my body.

Plus, endorphins make everybody happy, and who doesn't want to be happy? After researching all the options for gyms in the area, I finally worked up the courage to try out a free class at the local gym. Everyone seemed friendly, even if I felt my soul leave my body during what was supposed to be a scaled-down version of everyone else's workout. And yet, despite the brutal workouts, I still found it in me to drag myself back to the gym at least three times a week.

Logan often attended the evening classes while I went to the morning class since I work evening shifts. However, he would drop into the morning class from time to time. It was hard not to notice Logan since he would often take off his shirt during the workouts. I'm woman enough to admire an attractive and fit man, so different from the last guy I dated who had a "dad bod."

At some point, we ended up chatting after workouts. During the holiday party hosted at the gym, we ended up talking the whole time and connecting. We started casually dating, but within a few months, he asked me to move in with him since my lease with my college roommates was ending, anyway. Initially, he disliked my two rescued kittens and relegated them to the deep bowels of the basement of the apartment, but he eventually warmed up to them.

I was so happy to start a healthy relationship with someone I thought had good morals and was a stand-up guy.

Our relationship was so smooth. I can't even recall any singular event or fight we ever had. We always just... got along. I enjoyed our quiet moments together just as much as our conversations.

I thought he loved me, but it felt like I was talking to a completely different person than the Logan I knew and loved when he told me he needed me to move out of his apartment. He felt cold and detached. Robotic. It's as if he just turned off his emotions to me, and I'm left in the dark without direction.

Sigh.

It's still New Year's Day, and I have yet to set my obligatory resolution. After the mess that was the last twenty-four hours, if there is one thing I was certain of, it was that I refuse to put myself in a situation that makes me unsafe or uncomfortable just to fit into Logan's timeline. By his own account, he has had months to come to terms with his decision, while I haven't even had a day to figure out the next step.

Logan can suck it until I find a suitable living arrangement. He can sleep in the guest bedroom or on the couch for all I care.

I sit up with determination and make a New Year's resolution: this year will be the year for me. It will be the first time I've been single in years, and I am going to enjoy every second. I want to meet new people and enjoy new experiences. Maybe I'll even try some one-night stands to see how I like it since I have never had one before.

Yes, this year will be for me and only me.

But first, I think I need to find a roommate.

4
Emily

It's been two weeks of trying to find a suitable roommate. So far, I've called in all the help I can get between my friends, their friends, and my coworkers. I even tried to find people I went to high school with whom I heard were looking for a roommate, but the timing of when they needed to move didn't line up with the urgency of mine.

While I had been searching online for apartments, my *gracious* ex-boyfriend was kind enough to ask around for any helpful leads for anyone subletting their homes. Luckily, one of his cop buddies knew of a vacancy in town with the earliest move-in date of February 1st. That meant I had about four more weeks to find a roommate, or I would have to move in alone for a while and eat ramen every day just to afford the rent.

The good news about the apartment was that it was in a nice, trendy town known for its social life. And while I have had zero luck finding a roommate, I'm excited to get out of my current situation and start the next chapter in my life.

Logan and I have been keeping things as amicable as possible. We barely see each other anymore, which helps relieve any awkwardness. When we run into each other, it's strictly business. I've since moved into the guest bedroom, and the cats have followed me there too, obviously.

I just got off the phone with my best friend from college, Sasha, who was my roommate before I moved in with Logan. It's her birthday celebration tonight, and she wanted to make sure that I was still planning on going. I thought about bailing and spending the night in since I'm not in the mood to be social lately, but Sasha was hard to turn down.

Besides, seeing some friendly faces and letting loose a little would be nice. I've been feeling on edge with everything lately. It's like I'm waiting for the next shoe to drop.

That's it. I need to get out of this headspace and try to think positively.

I think a new outfit for tonight's activities will help lift my spirits.

♥ ♥ ♥ ♥ ♥

I show up to the bar for Sasha's birthday celebration in my new outfit, which includes a cute top and tight-fitting jeans paired with black lace-up combat boots. I feel more like myself than I have been in a couple of weeks, and it feels so good.

I find my friends crowded around a table at the bar and saunter up to them. When they notice me, I cringe at the shrieks of excitement that I actually showed up. I guess I had everyone worried about being a no-show tonight with everything going on.

After a round of hugs, I'm offered a drink and sit at the table. As I'm chatting and catching up with my friends, I notice Amanda brought not only her husband, Jason, but I spot his best friend, Ben, at the bar with him. I've known Ben for as long as Amanda and Jason have been together, which has been about five years. They met in college and got married a couple of years ago. They're married now and expecting their first baby soon.

Last I heard from Amanda, Ben had just broken off his engagement with his long-term girlfriend in October and was living with them for the time being. I feel a pang of sympathy for his predicament, which seems eerily similar to mine.

As I'm talking to Amanda, it strikes me that this could solve my current problem. I can't help but ask Amanda if Ben has had any luck finding a place to live.

"No, he hasn't really found a place yet. He's still in our guest bedroom, but I'm not sure how long he plans to stay. The baby is due in the springtime, you know?" Amanda says, a little frown marring her perfect complexion.

I pause before I pose the next question as nonchalantly as I can muster.

"Do you think he would move in with me? I have an apartment, but I need a roommate in order to make it work."

Amanda's eyes widen with excitement.

"Oh my god, I bet he would! That would work out so perfectly! If he moves in with you, we can get the nursery set up for the baby faster! Let's go ask him!"

"Wait!" I stop her from running off to talk to Ben. "Let me ask him when he comes over."

And give me more time to work up the nerve to figure out what to say to him.

It isn't until maybe twenty minutes later that Jason and Ben rejoin our group, at which point Ben and I exchange polite greetings.

Ben has always been nice to me, but we rarely see each other despite sharing mutual friends. The few times I had seen him, he was always with his now ex-fiancée, Melissa. I've tried to make Melissa feel included anytime she was around, but I always got the sense that she was insecure and jealous of our group of girls.

The last time I saw Ben, I had just heard news of his engagement to Melissa. He seemed less than enthused about the prospect, but now it makes sense that the engagement didn't last.

After several minutes of catching up with the group, I finally worked up the courage to turn to Ben, who perks up with interest at my renewed attention.

"So, I heard you're staying with Amanda and Jason right now." I idly pick at the label of the beer bottle, the cold glass cool against my palm. A restless energy vibrates beneath my skin.

"Yeah, I guess everyone knows at this point." He chuckles as a hand reaches up to run through his dark hair.

"I'm sorry to hear about what happened with you and Melissa."

Ben just shrugs and takes a sip out of his cold beer.

"How's apartment hunting?" My palms are sweating as I prepare to present the proposal devised to solve our issues.

"Honestly, I've been so busy with work that I have had little time to look. I know Amanda can't wait to get me out of their house with the new baby coming, so I'll have to figure out something soon," he replies.

I nod, listening intently, though I had already known based on what Amanda had just told me. I clear my throat and try to ignore the anxiety churning in my gut.

"So... my boyfriend and I just broke up, and I actually found a nice apartment, but I need a roommate..."

He raises one eyebrow for me to continue.

"Do you... Do you want to move in with me? I mean, as a roommate?" I bite down on my lower lip, letting the question hang heavily in the air between us.

He stares at me for several seconds, his eyes bouncing between mine. I blush at the intensity of his gaze.

"Sure," he finally says.

"I mean... it would be temporary... Wait, are you sure?"

"Yeah. I'll move in with you."

I'm taken aback by his straightforward response.

"Do you... Do you want to think about it before giving me an answer?" I ask, even though I mentally slap myself, knowing I need this to work out.

"No, I'm good."

"I have cats," I warn.

"I love cats," he answers.

"Well... okay then."

"Okay, roomie." He taps his beer to mine, takes a swig of his beer, and winks at me.

That went much easier than I had thought it would.

I think I feel my heart skip a beat, but I blame it on indigestion.

5
Ben

My feet strike the pavement in a calming rhythm as my breath evens out. There is nothing compared to the runner's high once I get going. These days, I've been running more frequently as part of a competition with the guys on my team at work. I'm determined to win the upcoming race.

It's been nice to have something to focus on ever since my life imploded so spectacularly. Though it was absolutely necessary, it doesn't help the sting I still feel at having to walk away from Melissa. The moment I broke off our engagement, her face contorted in a mask of betrayal, a mixture of hurt, anger, and disbelief etched in every line of her features. It remains etched in my memory.

I never should have let things go for as long as it did. A mistake I'll never make again. I knew Melissa and I were wrong for each other, but I was young. And stupid. It was also easier to fall into a relationship than always putting myself out there to be rejected. I wasted both of our time, and there is no way to take it back.

Living with Jason and Amanda has been a pleasant break from the reality of my life. Jason has been a great friend to me since our irresponsible college days. Though he was a couple of years older than me, he had been doing the "five-year plan" at college. We've bailed one another out more times than I can count. I like to think that if not for my help, Jason would not have graduated college with me.

He landed a job at the biggest firm in the state. I'm sure his father working at the company helped. Nepotism at its best, but I can't complain. Jason's father's influence at the company extended to me during the selection process, too. I've worked my ass off to rise to the top of the ranks over the past decade to prove my worth ever since.

Work has been my priority for so long. Melissa working for the same company also made things easier. She knew the level of dedication that was required to climb the corporate ladder. It wasn't an issue until I had an epiphany about how unhappy we made each other.

We had been together for years before I proposed. For months, she'd been hinting at wanting to get married; then, after a terrible fight, I bought a ring. I gave her the ring as a token of my commitment. I had hoped it would make her happy. And it seemed to have worked for a short time. My grand gesture bought me a couple of months of Melissa's seemingly genuine happiness, but the sweetness of that time eventually faded, replaced by the bitter taste of our unresolved issues.

Melissa wanted the white-picket fence with the two-and-a-half kids and a dog. While I had known what she wanted, I mistakenly thought we also shared the same professional aspirations. The thought of having kids at our age seemed daunting. I wasn't ready for it.

And, if I were being honest, I couldn't see myself with her for the rest of my life. Melissa was often jealous of any woman, regardless of the fact that I would never cheat on her. She would start fights over the smallest perceived grievance, and it became exhausting.

When I didn't show any interest in the wedding planning, we

started fighting again. I reached my breaking point and called off the engagement. I moved out and into Jason and Amanda's home by the weekend.

That's where I've been for the past few months. I've buried myself in work and started running again.

I probably should have been working harder to find an apartment, but I didn't have it in me to admit to my failures.

Melissa still called me, hoping I would change my mind and move back in. Though I knew it was a mistake, I had agreed to meet her at the apartment a few weeks ago. It had been uncomfortable at first. I tried to keep my distance, but knowing she was hurting because of me wore me down. One thing led to another, and the next thing I knew, we were in the bedroom.

The disgust I felt at what I allowed to happen was immeasurable. As I got dressed to leave, Melissa started crying. I'm not sure what she had hoped to gain from us sleeping together, but I clearly wasn't giving it to her. I've been careful to avoid seeing her again despite receiving multiple calls from her begging me to come over.

I round the corner as Jason and Amanda's home comes into view. The sun is setting behind me, and I still need to shower and get ready. Apparently, I have plans tonight with some of Amanda's friends.

I don't mind being social, but I'd much rather stay in and catch up on some work. When Amanda informed us about the plans, Jason's eyes lit up with excitement when he turned to me and invited me to go. They've done so much for me in the past few months, and I could use a break.

It will be nice to let loose for one night.

♥ ♥ ♥ ♥ ♥

The bar is noisy and crowded. It feels nice to be surrounded by people enjoying themselves. Jason is telling me some wild story about something that happened to him earlier in the week, as if he hasn't already told me the same story at least three times since. I nod politely and look around the bar.

Amanda and some of her friends are sitting at a table in the corner. I can see her chatting with the birthday girl, Sasha, animatedly as Sasha nods along. The scene seems eerily similar to my current situation, and I bite back a smile. Jason and Amanda met at a bar a few years ago. According to Jason, it had been love at first sight. They'd hit it off on the dance floor and have been inseparable since.

My eyes catch sight of a familiar dark-haired beauty. I haven't seen her in a while, but every time, I swear I feel my heart skip a beat. Emily is standing at the doorway, looking for her friends. I watch as her face lights up at spotting her friends. She seems radiant tonight, with her dark hair flowing down her back.

I watch as she moves gracefully between the crowd of people and greets her friends. I'm too far away to hear them, but I imagine their excited shrieks at seeing the newcomer. It makes me wonder if she's still with that loser. Kevin? Kyle? Some hotshot cop who thought his shit didn't stink.

Emily deserves someone better than her loser boyfriend. I felt it was not my place to say anything, considering I had been with Melissa ever since I met Emily. Though I always kept a respectful distance from her, I couldn't help but feel drawn to her. Every time she entered the room, I felt the energy shift. She was magnetic, and I was helpless to orbit around her.

It seems her friends feel the same shift as they all delightedly crowd around her. I try to be discreet and not openly stare, but I can't help but watch her every move. She is mesmerizing to watch. From the way she shyly tucks an errant strand of hair behind her ears to the way her smile reaches her eyes, making the corners crinkle.

Finally, Jason seemed to notice where my attention had gone.

"Oh, good, she came!" Jason motions for the bartender to grab another round of beers and settle their tab.

I see Emily glance over at them a couple of times and hide a smirk behind my hand. It seems she also notices them at the bar. They make their way through the crowd to the table. I give everyone a nod in greeting and grab the seat at the head of the table while Jason sits down next to his wife.

After a few minutes, I sense Emily's attention on me. Turning to face her, I watch as she plays with the label on her drink.

Whatever I expected, it certainly wasn't the news of her and that loser, Logan, breaking up. Who would be stupid enough to let her go? Her next words caught me completely off guard.

"Do you... Do you want to move in with me? I mean, as a roommate?"

It seems logical she'd need a roommate, and as it helps me too, I don't give it much consideration. I watch in fascination as a blush creeps up her neck, my eyes roaming her face as I pretend to think it over.

"Sure." I try to play it cool.

"I mean... it would be temporary... Wait, are you sure?" Her sweet voice is the only thing I can hear despite the crowded bar.

"Yeah. I'll move in with you." I play it cool and shrug, though the earth feels like it is moving beneath my feet.

At best, I can move out of Jason and Amanda's home, and they can get the nursery ready for the baby. At worst... Well, actually, I can't think of a worst-case scenario.

"Do you... Do you want to think about it before giving me an answer?" She wrings her hands nervously.

"No, I'm good." My voice is firm. I've already made up my mind.

"I have cats," she says warily.

"I love cats." It's true. Melissa had two Persian cats, and I miss their companionship more than I'd like to admit.

"Well... okay then," she says with finality.

"Okay, roomie." I tap my beer on hers, gulping the bitter taste of it. I shoot her a playful wink.

This is going to be great. I just know it.

6

Emily

I woke up feeling hopeful this morning. After what feels like a constant string of bad luck, I'm finally getting my feet back under me. Feeling the world spin out of control has been a dreadful, disorienting experience, and I've struggled to regain my bearings. Since New Year's Eve, I felt trapped on the endlessly rotating merry-go-round, the relentless motion making me feel sick as I unsuccessfully searched for a way off of the nightmarish ride.

In all honesty, the subtle cracks in my life had been widening for months, like a slow, silent collapse, while I remained blissfully unaware, my head buried in the sand. I stubbornly avoided acknowledging the glaring red flags that ultimately caused my longest relationship to fail.

With the start of the year came a new perspective, and I revisited my interactions with Logan over the past few months, filtering them through this newfound clarity. A month or so ago, we were hanging out with his coworker and his wife; she and I had become friends. Something felt off, but I thought I was overreacting. Later, I asked Logan if anything seemed off. He acted like everything was fine and ignored my worries. Looking back,

I wonder if he'd told his friends he was going to dump me before he actually did.

The strong vibrations of Spike's comforting purr help me focus on the present moment. I give him a gentle pet and scratch him under his chin in appreciation. Buffy is snoring softly by my feet.

I rescued Buffy and Spike when they were kittens. I was scrolling on Facebook when I came across a post from someone I went to high school with, asking if anyone was looking to adopt any kittens. Someone had dropped off their litter of kittens in a duct-taped plastic storage container with crude air holes in front of a pet store.

I was a broke nursing student, but having just gotten out of an emotionally abusive relationship, I felt a pang of sympathy for the plight of these poor kittens. Within hours of seeing the post, I was already at the pet store, which was an hour away from where I lived.

I picked Buffy first as she was the runt of the litter, and I've always had a soft spot for the underdog, or underkitten, if you will. While playing with all the kittens, I kept picking kittens others had already claimed. They were all friendly and cute, and I knew I would not be walking out with just one. Since I spend many hours studying either at my apartment or at the library on campus, I wanted to make sure my feline friends had at least each other for company.

Just as I was about to admit defeat, a small gray and white tuxedo kitten came slowly over to me. He had been sitting in the corner while I was playing with his littermates. He didn't seem inclined to leave his corner until then.

I felt a connection to the poor guy. He seemed shy and skittish. I knew he would need extra love and attention to come out of his shell. If nothing else, I knew that nobody could love him more than me.

I was right about Spike, whom I named after my favorite vampire from a popular TV show. He disliked being held or petted. He was almost always hiding while his sister, whose namesake arose from the same show, ran around exploring her new world fearlessly.

The only time Spike came out of his hiding place was when I was sleeping. When he finally worked up the courage to approach me, he always came to tuck his head in my hands. I'd wake up to him demanding that I pet him every night for months until he became more comfortable asking for affection when I was awake.

They are a few years old now and have been my constant companions. I graduated from nursing school last year and have been at the same nursing job in a busy and overwhelming medical-surgical unit for the past year.

Yawning, I try to stretch carefully so I don't accidentally dislodge Spike from his perch. Despite my strategic maneuvering, he gets up in a huff and lays down next to me.

I grab my phone and see that I slept in until 10 a.m. Checking my messages, I see that Ben and I had exchanged numbers last night so we could keep in contact.

Since we're going to be roommates, after all.

Groaning, I roll over and decide to send him another message now that we're both sober, even though I only had one drink last night. I didn't see Ben with more than a couple of drinks the whole time, either.

"Hey, Ben! It's Emily. Are you still okay with being roommates?"

I hit send and try not to think too hard about how my message might come across.

I get up to use the bathroom and wash up for the day. My plans today comprise packing, cleaning, and avoiding Logan as much as possible since I know it's also his day off today. Normally, we would get up together to make breakfast, but ever since he told me he didn't love me anymore, I've felt uncomfortable around him.

My phone vibrates as I get a new message. It's from Ben, and

I feel my heart race a little at seeing his name flash across the screen. I open up my messages to see his response.

"Yep! Still good to be roomies ;)"

Winky face? Is he flirting with me with emojis? My cheeks flush with the possibility. I've always found Ben attractive, but he has always been with Melissa, so I never thought of him as anything other than a mutual friendly acquaintance.

"Just wanted to mention again that I have 2 cats. Are you okay with living with cats?"

This is the deal breaker, for sure. I needed to know that whoever I lived with next would be cat-friendly. Even though Logan eventually warmed up to my two shadows, it took a while before he let them go upstairs into our bedroom. It was so hard for me to not have my sleeping buddies, but since I was the one who moved into Logan's space, I didn't want to upset him. The cats eventually won him over, though.

"I love cats," he replies.

Well, okay then. This is really happening. I didn't realize how anxious I was until I let out a big breath. I guess a part of me just thought that it was too good to be true. After struggling to find an affordable apartment, one just fell into my lap, albeit because of selfish motivations on Logan's part, but I am not about to look a gift horse in the mouth. Then, after days of trying to find a roommate, Ben agrees with no questions.

I can't help but feel like maybe this year wouldn't be so terrible after all.

7

Emily

I'm sitting in my car outside of the new apartment while reading the latest fantasy romance book by my favorite author on my Kindle, waiting for Ben. It's actually a split-level home, and we will rent out the second floor of the house. It boasts two bedrooms and a modest-sized kitchen, with laundry hookups in the basement, but the best part about the apartment is the four-season sunroom.

I envision myself practicing yoga all year long in the room that faces the street. I've seen pictures of the apartment, but today will be the first time touring the place and, hopefully, signing the lease if everything looks good.

Ben is on his way from work to meet me so we can go through everything together. Outside of discussing the details of the apartment and when we can meet, we have not really been talking.

After the tour and signing of the lease today, we made plans to go to happy hour down the street to celebrate. Our new apartment is within walking distance of the town's trendiest bars, restaurants, and boutique shops, which makes me so excited at the prospect of having more opportunities to meet new people.

Who knows, maybe I'll finally have my first one-night stand.

I see a car pulling up from down the street and notice that it's Ben behind the wheel. When he notices me, he smiles brightly as our eyes connect. I'm blindsided momentarily by the sheer joy on his face as he looks at me. I smile shyly in greeting. Suddenly, I feel a flock of butterflies swarming my belly.

I've never had this type of response to Ben before, so it's a little unsettling, considering we're about to make an enormous commitment together.

We will need to establish ground rules to prevent hurt feelings when the lease ends.

I'm getting out of my car just as Ben parks his across the street. I wait for him by the sidewalk as he hurries to meet me. He shines his dazzling smile at me again before opening his arms to me.

"I'm not sure if we should hug or shake hands since we're about to be roomies." He chuckles.

"Um… we can hug, I guess." Before I can even finish my sentence, I feel his arms come around me. It's a friendly hug, but having not felt any affection in months now, it's still a shock to my system. Logan and I had stopped being intimate months ago. I never realized that we also stopped with our casual touches, too, until this moment.

Wow. It seems I still have a lot of issues to work through.

I clear my throat and gesture to the front door.

"We should probably go inside."

He follows closely behind me as I ring the doorbell. I feel the warmth of his body heat against my back and shiver involuntarily. Even though it's mid-January and freezing out, I feel flushed suddenly.

The door opens, and a stout elderly woman is on the other side of the door. She has a scowl on her face as she looks us over. We must pass her visual inspection because she stands aside to let us in without saying a word.

After we shut the door and enter, she leads us up the spiral wooden staircase; a man who seems to be in his fifties is waiting in the kitchen doorway.

He greets us with a warm smile and introduces himself as the landlord's son, Aleks. I'm assuming the elderly woman is to be our landlord. He has a thick Polish accent as he guides us through the small yet cozy apartment.

I am in love with the space and can picture myself living here. I look over at Ben, who is keenly looking over the space. Our eyes collide, and I wonder what he's thinking.

Aleks walks us back into the kitchen, where several documents are sitting on the counter. He goes over the details of the lease, as well as the deposits required to hold the space and monthly rent costs. He reviews the utilities included and then looks up at us expectantly.

I'm reaching for the pen in Alek's hand, ready to sign the lease when I hear Ben clear his throat.

"Actually, Aleks, I just have a few questions…"

I glance over at Ben, startled, as he asks Aleks basic questions like when rent is due, which I should have thought to ask myself. Feeling silly, I sit there quietly as I listen to their conversation.

Thank goodness Ben took over the situation.

As their conversation dies down, Aleks hands the pen over to Ben, who signs without hesitation. He then looks up at me and smirks, slowly passing the pen over to me to sign the leasing documents.

"You sure you're ready for this?"

I swallow nervously as I grab the pen from his hand. Our fingers barely make contact, but I swear I feel an electric thrill passing between us. Judging by the lack of change in Ben's expression, I figured it was in my head.

"As ready as I'll ever be."

With a decisive stroke of my pen, I sign my name, the ink a dark contrast against the crisp white paper. A legally binding contract, sealed with ink and promises, intertwines our lives for the foreseeable future.

8
Emily

Aleks walks us out of the apartment after we have signed all the documents. Our move-in date isn't until February 1st, so we still have a few weeks to pack and get ready.

Ben and I are standing on the sidewalk when we turn to face each other. We're both smiling eagerly at the next step in moving on with our lives.

"So, do you still want to go to happy hour now?" I ask tentatively.

"Sure. Lead the way." Ben gestures for me to go ahead of him as he falls into step beside me.

I pull up the map on my phone to navigate us to Billy's, a bar that's famous for its happy hour deals with cheap, delicious food and fantastic drinks.

It's only about a five-minute walk. Ben and I walk side by side in comfortable silence as we look around at our soon-to-be neighborhood. As we turn the corner, I notice he switches sides so that he's the one closest to the street, but I think nothing of it as we make our way to the restaurant.

Once we get there, the hostess informs us we can just seat ourselves at the bar. We find the only two seats available at the large counter. I'm taking off my coat when I feel his hands on my shoulders. Startled, I look over my shoulder, but he simply raises his eyebrow. He helps me take off my coat, hanging it on my chair as he pulls it out and motions for me to sit.

His excellent manners surprise me, and my cheeks heat as I take my seat. Ben removes his coat and claims the seat next to me as I look around at the bar. The vibe is cozy chic, and the patrons seem like corporate millennials who are all dressed to impress. I feel out of place in my jeggings, oversized sweater, and ankle boots.

Ben seems to fit in with the crowd in his button-down collared shirt tucked into gray slacks that seem to fit him perfectly. He's even wearing a tie to finish the look. I was never into corporate-type guys, and Logan was always either in his uniform or in gym clothes.

Ben hands me the happy hour menu, and we're both quiet as we look over the options.

Our eyes meet over the menu, and I feel a tingle rush down my spine.

"Do you know what you want?" I ask him after a moment.

He pauses before he finally answers, "Yeah, I think I do."

I don't think he's talking about what's on the menu for tonight.

The bartender comes over to us to take our order, and we both order a drink and some food. Normally, the prices are almost double for the food and drinks, but since it's happy hour, we're able to get everything at a steep discount.

No complaints here.

As the bartender walks away, we both turn to each other.

I get nervous thinking that small talk would be difficult with Ben since I've always struggled with it. Call me borderline anti-social, but I always found small talk to be tedious. I would rather spend my free time reading or at the gym most days, where talking is impossible since it's imperative to keep breathing through a rough workout.

Surprisingly, Ben is so easy to talk to and puts me at ease with his calm and friendly demeanor.

At some point, we've both turned our bodies so that we're facing each other, our knees naturally making room for the other person without effort. I don't take too much time to think about how well we seem to fit together, like two pieces of a puzzle.

After a lull in the conversation, Ben looks me over.

"I never asked you before, but how are you doing?" I look up at him as I ponder his question. I don't think he's asking it in a friendly way but more so to get a sense of where my head is post-Logan.

"You know Logan and I broke up…" He tips his chin down in affirmation. "Well, I guess I'm single now and just trying to figure things out."

Ben takes a moment to absorb my answer before responding. "For what it's worth, he never deserved you."

I give him a small smile. "Thanks."

I've been hearing that a lot lately.

As we sit there sipping on our drinks, I fidget. I'm wrestling with the urge to just come out and ask him about how he ended up single at the bar with me. I take a big gulp of my cocktail and work up the nerve to ask him.

"Can I ask…" When he doesn't stop me, it gives me the courage to continue my line of questioning, "What happened between you and Melissa? Last time I saw you, before Sasha's birthday party, you guys were engaged…"

His demeanor seems to change from happy and relaxed to tense and guarded in the blink of an eye.

"Melissa and I… We were together for so long. We had a lot of issues, but we were both unhappy. I knew she wanted me to propose. I thought it would make her happy…" He takes a sip from his beer before continuing. "We just weren't the right fit."

I'm nodding as I take in his answer. I always thought that Logan and I fit together so well, like two peas in a pod. We always just got along and coasted through life. I never expected to be single at thirty years old and living with a roommate at this stage in my life.

"I have an idea."

Ben looks at me with his eyebrow cocked.

"How about we be each other's wingperson? You know, I'll be your wingwoman, and you be my wingman, and we help each other get dates or whatever?" Saying it out loud sounded so ridiculous, but how else will we both get out from under our exes and past relationships?

Isn't that how that saying goes? The best way to get over someone is to get under someone else? Why not have a partner in crime while doing it and also someone to make sure the other person is safe?

He takes a moment to answer, but then he's smiling at me like I'm a genius, and it does things to me I refuse to acknowledge.

"Sure, I'll be your wingman." He winks at me before turning back to his food, which arrived while we were chatting.

9

Emily

The last few weeks passed by in a whirlwind as I finished packing and preparing all of my belongings to prepare for today. Move-in day. It just so happens that the day I'm moving out, Logan is stuck working a double shift, which means we won't have to maneuver around him as my friends help me load up the rental truck I borrowed for the day.

Luckily, one of my coworkers, Brittany, was getting rid of some barely used furniture. She sold me a new bed frame and a matching dresser set at a steep discount. Moving and furnishing an apartment wasn't in my budget, so I appreciated any money I could save. Brittany's been a friend of mine since we started training to work in the intensive care unit together last month. So, not only did I have to plan to move out of my home for the past three years, but I was also taking on a new job, which included rigorous training and hours of studying.

Yeah. I was feeling a little haggard these days.

But the day has finally arrived. I'm so busy packing everything and getting ready that I barely have time to think, much less eat. I want to get my things out of Logan's space as quickly as humanly possible.

The cats are already in their carriers and whining in my car.

They hate car rides with a passion. We have everything except for one dresser loaded into the truck since it was much too big to fit. Logan mentioned that if there was anything that I needed help with, he would help. I can't help but roll my eyes at his offer to get rid of me and out of his space. The least he could do was move the one piece of furniture we couldn't fit in the truck.

Things had been pretty awkward the past couple of weeks as we neared my move-in date. We avoided each other as much as possible, and when we were at home together, we were rarely in the same room. I locked myself up in the guest bedroom with the cats to study most of the time. I started eating my meals in the guest room instead of at the dinner table.

I don't know if it's because I have been so busy with all the changes happening in my life, but after the first couple of days when Logan first broke up with me, I've rarely cried over our failed relationship. Mostly, I've felt crushing disappointment at how things ended.

It also makes me sad at how quickly we went from friends to strangers. My relationship with Logan may be over, but he had been my best friend during our time together. I just feel that we won't be able to remain friends in the end.

Especially not right now when everything is still raw.

We're loading the last box into the medium-sized U-Haul I rented for today when it hits me that this will be the last time I'll be in this apartment. I walk back inside to do a final walk-through to make sure I missed nothing. Silently saying goodbye to the place that had been my home for years. Our laughter and happy memories echo within these walls.

I stare angrily at the couch, the place where Logan dumped me. My fingers trace the small table where we shared countless breakfasts. I tap the table lightly one last time, feeling the smooth surface under my fingertips, before walking out the door. As the door clicks shut, a sense of finality settles over me, mirroring the complex emotions that are swirling inside of me as I close this chapter. Leaving all the memories behind.

❤ ❤ ❤ ❤ ❤

It was probably ambitious of my friends and me to think we could simultaneously move out of one space and into a new apartment, on the second level, no less, on the same day. We vastly underestimated the time needed to finish everything today.

The cats and I were the first to step foot in the apartment. It's officially our place now. A strange mix of happiness and sorrow washes over me. After getting Buffy and Spike settled inside my walk-in closet, I shut the door and follow the sounds of voices. Sasha, Amanda, and Nikki were downstairs unpacking the truck while Jason and Chris were handling the heavier furniture. We have a lot of work ahead of us.

After a few hours of unpacking the truck, I make a quick stop at the local supermarket and pick up pizza and beer to thank my friends and their partners for all their help. I don't know if I could ever express my gratitude to them for just being here to help me during my time of need.

Ben isn't at our apartment yet. He mentioned he needed to get a new mattress delivered, and it won't arrive until this weekend. There didn't seem to be much sense for him to move in when there wasn't anywhere for him to sleep yet.

We've kept in touch over the past few weeks and even met to go shopping for couches. Ultimately, the local discount furniture store was our best course of action. We scored a leather sectional and matching loveseat, coffee table, and some decor for under a grand. The store discounted the furniture because of imperfections or damages, but these were insignificant or easily concealed with a blanket. For the space and the price, it was well worth the cost. The downside to shopping at the discount furniture store is that they don't deliver, so we have to move the furniture ourselves.

Ben and Jason made plans to pick up the items later on in the week.

In the meantime, I'm staying at the new apartment by myself for the first couple of nights. Since it's in a safe neighborhood and being on the second floor, I'm not too nervous about it. I try hard not to think about the fact that it's the first time I've been alone in years.

It's getting late, and we're just putting the last pieces of my bed frame together before my friends say goodbye. I'm given tight hugs and firm statements to "call if you need anything" before they all leave.

I'm finally alone.

I keep busy by making up my new bed and start unpacking. I went out and splurged on a new bedsheet set to mark the occasion. Fresh sheets for a fresh start and all that.

I walk through the apartment, locking the front and back doors. I even check the windows for good measure. After securing everything, I wash up and get ready for bed.

I'm tucking myself into bed before the tears fall. The heavy weight of loneliness, a leaden pressure in my chest, finally pushed me over the edge.

I lay there, tears falling silently, as I finally let the events of the past six weeks catch up to me. My heart aches with the loss of my relationship. It was devastating to come to terms with the fact that I had lost the place I had cherished as home for years. Even acknowledging Logan's flaws, losing my best friend still devastates me.

I know everything happens for a reason, but at this moment, I'm finding it hard to find the reason my life imploded so spectacularly.

10
Emily

Ben texted he was bringing the furniture and asked me to unlock the door so he and Jason could bring it inside. I rush through the apartment to make sure that the guys have enough space to bring the furniture in. I spent the better part of the weekend unpacking my things and trying to make the space feel like a home. Unfortunately, there are boxes and random crap strewn about everywhere.

When Ben and Jason finally show up, I'm a sweaty mess. I open the front door for them as they unload the truck they borrowed. As I wave to Ben and Jason in greeting, I feel my phone vibrate.

I pull out my phone to see that I have a text from Logan telling me he's on the way to the apartment with the dresser that I couldn't fit in my truck. Of course, Logan just expects me to be here waiting for him. Unfortunately for him, I have to head out for my hair appointment shortly, and I'm not missing it just because Logan dropped by unannounced. I leave him on read and tuck my phone into the side pocket of my leggings.

Ben and Jason have the couch balanced between them, and they slowly make their way to the front door. I make eye contact with Ben, and we smile at each other in greeting.

"Morning, roomie," Ben says to me as he makes his way past me.

"Oh, hey, roomie," I say back to him. My voice comes out a little too breathy to me.

I follow them up the stairs to the apartment so they can deposit the couch in its rightful place in the living room.

"Are you guys good without me? I have to leave in a minute for my hair appointment." Ben nods at me. I let him know Logan is dropping by with my dresser while I'm out. His gaze scours my face at the news. I'm not sure what he sees, but after a moment, he nods tersely.

"Just tell Logan to leave it in the dining room until I can make space for it in my bedroom," I instruct as I head out to leave.

"You got it, boss," Ben replies as I walk out the door.

I turn around and give him a wave, and he gives me a sarcastic salute. I ignore the way my stomach does a nervous flip-flop at his playful gesture.

♡ ♡ ♡ ♡ ♡

I'm sitting at the salon where Maria, my hairdresser and best friend, is in the process of coloring my hair when I feel my phone vibrate with a text message. We went bold and added some blonde and caramel highlights to my otherwise naturally dark hair. I've tried to go blonde once, and it didn't go well with my caramel complexion. Plus, I found I didn't have more fun as a blonde than I did as a brunette.

I look at my phone and find a notification that Logan has sent me a few messages.

"I met your roommate."

"You didn't tell me your new roommate was a guy."

"Are you seriously living with another dude already?"

"WTF, Emily."

"How much do you really know about that guy?"

"Answer me."

I frown as I read his messages. I guess I never told him about my new living arrangements, but since he had been acting like an emotionless robot ever since he broke things off with me, I assumed he didn't care or needed to know.

He can't be… jealous about it, can he? I mean, I guess it's a possibility, and it makes me feel a little sense of relief to know that if he is jealous, then that means he didn't completely stop caring for me.

"I guess you met Ben." I hit send and then put my phone away. Although, technically, he knows Ben from past house parties, they've only exchanged pleasantries, so it's not like Ben is a complete stranger to him.

Looking up, I make eye contact with Maria in the mirror. I've already told her the entire story, so she's up to date with my life. I first met Maria at the gym, and she has been there since the start. She's seen our relationship develop from a crush into a relationship. She's witnessing it falling apart now, too.

"That was Logan. He just met my roommate."

Maria just nods and hums. She continues to wrap my hair in foil before meeting my eyes in the mirror.

"I need to tell you something." Her serious tone makes me sit up straighter in her chair.

"What? What is it?" My heart is pounding in anticipation of her words.

"Logan called me on New Year's." She speaks slowly, giving me time to process what she said.

"He called you? Why?" Since we all became friends at the same time, their conversations weren't an unusual occurrence.

"He told me that he broke up with you and wanted me to know so that I could help you…" Her voice trails off, and she raises a brow at me.

"Help me? Help me with what?" My voice comes out louder than I intended, echoing through the otherwise empty studio.

"He wanted to see if I could help you move out of his place."

"Are you kidding me?"

"No, and let me tell you, I was not happy with how he handled things. And I let him know."

The thought of Maria chewing Logan out made me cringe, but it was comforting to have an ally. I guess that means I got Maria in the divorce.

"Logan is a douchebag," Maria says with finality.

"Yeah, he fucking sucks."

I agree as I slump back into my chair. I'm reeling from Logan's betrayal. Before I could tell our friends, he'd already started figuring out how to get rid of me.

I know Maria has an opinion about my new living arrangements, but she's keeping those thoughts to herself for now. She doesn't know Ben, but she seemed genuinely shocked when I told her I was moving in with a boy.

I'm out of the salon in a couple of hours. My hair is lighter and brighter. I feel better already.

Getting in my car, I see a missed call from Logan and a text from Ben on my phone. I open up Ben's message first.

"Hey, don't know if you already have plans for dinner, but I'm gonna order a pizza for delivery in case you're hungry."

Well, that was thoughtful of him.

"I love pizza. Thank you, I appreciate it!" I type out the response and send it to him.

I turn on the car and call Logan back, though I regret it instantly. The dial tone rings loudly through the Bluetooth connection in my car. A sickening dread grips me as I hope he won't answer. Unfortunately, the phone call's loud connection rings filled my car.

"Emily, seriously. What the fuck? You're living with a guy? You don't even know him!"

I'm taken aback by the aggressive tone since he's never been this angry when we were together.

"It's not like I had much of a choice..." I say before he cuts me off.

"Are you kidding me right now? You should have told me you couldn't find a roommate. I would have given you more time if I had known you needed it! You never told me anything! You didn't need to move in with a stranger!" he yells.

I'm speechless and not sure how to respond to him. How was I supposed to tell him when he shut me out and was practically kicking me out the door? But now, because he finds out my roommate is a guy, he suddenly cares about me?

"Are you... Are you serious right now, Logan? Did you forget you tried to kick me out not even twenty-four hours after you broke up with me?"

"I did not kick you out..." Logan groans, and I can picture him rubbing the back of his neck in agitation.

"Or that I saw you were googling how to evict someone when you left your laptop open?"

"Listen, Emily, I'm sorry. You weren't supposed to see that..."

"Or, how about the fact that you called Maria before I could tell her to see if she'd take me in like a stray animal?" I'm fuming; a roaring sound fills my ears, and a bitter taste fills my mouth as the pent-up anger pours out of me. The nerve of him! Pretending to be the victim when his treachery had been unfolding right before my eyes this whole time.

I hear him let out a big sigh.

"I'm just... I'm just worried about you," Logan offers meekly.

"Well, you don't need to worry about me. I'm fine."

"You know I still care about you..."

"Do I?" I ask sarcastically.

"Of course I do. You've been my best friend for years..."

I tune him out as tears fall. I've been waiting weeks for him to show some emotions about our breakup and he chooses now to tell me.

"Yeah, well, you've been a shitty friend lately," I say spitefully.

"I know, babe... I mean... it's just..." He takes a deep breath. "I'm gonna get going. If you need anything..."

I hang up the phone without saying goodbye.

Fuck Logan. He didn't deserve another second of my time.

11
Ben

The couch is heavier than it looks. Jason leads the way as we maneuver the leather sleeper sofa off the moving truck. Emily pops her head out the door to greet and open the door for us.

"Morning, roomie," I shout as I pretend that the couch weighs nothing between the both of us. I don't hear her response as we make our way up the walkway.

We pause in the doorway, setting our load down carefully as we catch our breath. I know it's heavy if Jason is struggling with it. He's half a foot taller than me and built like a linebacker. We severely underestimated our ability to deliver our own furniture.

We stare up at the spiraling staircase, both of us wondering how the hell we are going to do it without taking out a chunk of the wall or hurting ourselves. I can't help but laugh at the situation. Jason looks over at me in confusion.

"Let's do this." I tilt my chin at Jason in a move that's meant to be encouraging. I wipe a hand across my brow at the sweat already gathering there despite the chilly weather.

Emily is hot on our heels as we wind our way up with our heavy cargo. I'm trying my best not to grunt as the couch snags a corner. With some angling, Jason and I are able to get the couch the rest of the way up the stairs.

Emily gestures to where she wants to place the couch, and I let out a quiet sigh of relief that it's not much further before I can drop the damn thing. Thank goodness it will be a while before I have to move it again. If all goes well, we have at least a year in the apartment before we have to worry about moving.

We place the couch in the corner of the living room, and I wipe my hands on my jeans and turn toward Emily, who is a vision in her tight black leggings and loose top.

"Are you guys good without me? I have to leave in a minute for my hair appointment." I glance over her face and nod, and she warns me about her ex-boyfriend stopping by with her furniture. "Just tell Logan to leave it in the corner of my bedroom for now."

"You got it, boss." I give her a mock salute at her command.

She laughs and turns away. I try not to pay attention to the way her butt looks in those tight pants. It should be illegal to have her prancing around the apartment wearing them. How am I supposed to keep things platonic when I just wanted to take a bite of her perky bottom?

It seems I may have underestimated my attraction to her.

"Dude, you're in so much trouble," Jason's voice breaks through my dirty thoughts.

I shoot him a glare and grab my water bottle. I don't bother answering him as he chuckles.

Jason and I discussed the implications of the move. I'm trying to ignore my attraction to my new roommate, and I know staying just friends won't be easy. Even though Jason is glad I moved on, it was fun to be his roommate again. It reminded me of our college days, but he is married and having a baby soon. Jason's life is on the verge of a transformation, and I won't interfere with his future.

I follow him back down the stairs to continue bringing in the rest of the furniture.

A few minutes later, as I'm setting up my bedroom for my new mattress, there's a loud knock on the door.

"Coming!" I shout as I make my way across the apartment and down the spiral staircase. Jason had just left. Thinking he had forgotten his phone or something, I yank open the door with a mocking smile on my face.

Only, it isn't Jason standing in the doorway, but a face I've come to loathe.

Logan.

I cross my arms across my bare chest and lean against the doorway.

"Can I help you?" My tone is mocking. I know why he's here, but it doesn't mean I have to make things easy for the spineless prick.

"What the hell are you doing here?" Logan's face reddens, his tone one of both shock and anger.

It looks like Emily didn't tell her loser ex-boyfriend who her new roommate was. I feel a genuine smile spread across my face.

"I live here."

"You live here?" His screech grates on my nerves.

"Yeah. What do you want?" I cock my eyebrow at him, wanting to get him off my property before Emily gets back.

Logan sputters for a moment before he regains his composure and gestures to his truck. I eye the large dresser on the back of it.

"Emily asked me to bring her dresser. Is she here?"

Logan's hopeful words at seeing Emily ignited a fire of rage inside of me as I recalled the way Logan had dumped her. Frustration burned as I clenched my fists against my chest, my arms and shoulders tensing, desperate to punch Logan. Logan was unworthy of sharing Emily's space, much less breathing the same air.

"No."

"I thought she would be here." His look of dejection pleased me.

65

"Sorry to disappoint. You can bring it upstairs."

I leave the door propped open as I make my way back up the stairs. I wasn't about to lift a finger to help the douchebag.

"Are you serious?" Logan yells at my retreating back.

A few minutes later, I hear the sound of two male voices. Looks like Logan called in for some help. I walk out into the living room to supervise as they bring in the dresser.

Taking a swig of my water, I gesture for the bumbling duo to bring the dresser into Emily's room. It sets me on edge seeing Logan in Emily's private space, but I will not make his life easier. No, the asshole deserves far worse than what is happening.

I chuckle at the sweat dripping down their faces as I lean casually against the wall. Crossing my arms as I direct them where to put the piece of furniture. Finally, when the dresser is where Emily requested, Logan and his buddy head toward the door to leave.

I'm hot on his tail when he stops at the top of the stairs.

"Joe, thanks for the help, man. I'll catch you later." Joe turns around and gives Logan a nod before disappearing down the stairs.

Facing me, Logan puffs out his chest, attempting to make himself seem bigger. I fight back a laugh as his attempt at intimidation falls completely flat.

"I don't know what your game is, but you better watch it," Logan spits his words out through clenched teeth.

Game? A moment of confusion gives way to clarity as I suddenly understand Logan's conclusions of the situation. His expression says it all. Though it is the wrong conclusion, I wanted to fuck with the dipshit.

"Your loss, my gain."

If the thought of Emily being with me makes Logan mad, then I'll play this game. After all, Logan is the idiot who dumped Emily. He deserves to sweat a little.

"That whore moved on fast."

"What did you call her?" My voice came out in a snarl.

A smirk plays on Logan's lips as he silently slips away, the shadows swallowing him whole. I listen to the click of the door as it echoes in the ensuing silence, clenching my fists as I wrestle with the urge to chase him down and punch him for what he said about Emily. The insult burns in my chest like an inferno. The only thing keeping my feet pinned to the floor is the thought of spending the rest of my life behind bars for attacking a police officer.

What a shame Emily couldn't see how her ex-boyfriend behaved. She still believes he is a good person despite how he's treated her. But, to me, he's just a jerk who treated her like his possession. Logan discarded Emily like a broken toy after he was done with her. A toy only he could play with.

Emily is more than just a possession.

I'll make sure she always knows that.

12

Emily

E ntering my new apartment, the delicious aroma of fresh pizza greets me. Ben has all the lights on in the apartment. It feels warm and inviting, a comforting sense of coziness filling the space. I caught my reflection in the rearview mirror before getting out of the car, and my eyes were still red and puffy from crying. Hopefully, Ben won't notice.

I hurry inside, shutting the door against the unusually harsh February chill. I take off my coat and shoes at the door and head upstairs, only to find Ben in the living room watching Netflix with a pizza. His warm smile greets me as I enter, instantly brightening my mood.

"Hey, roomie! Welcome home!"

I feel the corners of my mouth turn upward into an uncontrollable smile. Here I thought things might be awkward with Ben, but he's done nothing but be kind to me. I think we're going to get along just fine.

"Hey, Ben, thanks for getting pizza. I'll send you some money for it."

"Don't worry about it. Here, I grabbed a plate for you."

I head into the bathroom to wash my hands and return to a plate with pizza already served for me.

"What are you watching?" I ask him as I settle onto the loveseat opposite where he's sitting.

"Some historical documentary on Netflix." He looks over at me. Is he blushing? "I love history," he states with confidence.

"That's okay. I'm a nerd, too."

He lets out a laugh at my response.

Yeah, I think we'll get along just fine.

❦ ❦ ❦ ❦ ❦

W e hang out in companionable silence for an hour before he looks over at me and clears his throat. Glancing up at him, I raise my eyebrows in question.

"I saw your ex today."

"I'm sorry. I hope things weren't weird or anything…"

"It's fine…" he trails off before continuing, "He didn't seem too happy to see that I'm your roommate…"

"Yeah, I know. I talked to him afterward."

"Are you okay?" He looks worriedly at me.

"Yeah, I mean, it is what it is. He didn't ask, so I didn't tell him."

He says nothing for a while before he opens his mouth again to say, "I think he's still in love with you."

I scoff at him. "He has a funny way of showing it."

Getting up, I grab the dirty plates. I don't want to continue this conversation anymore. I'm getting emotional whiplash with Logan, and I am tired. Plus, Ben didn't even notice my new hair. I try not to let it bother me, but I thought I looked good.

I'm washing the dishes in the sink when I hear Ben come in with the empty pizza box. He takes care of the trash, and we head to our prospective bedrooms.

Our bedrooms share a single small hallway with the bathroom in the middle of both bedrooms. Ben heads into his room as I go into the bathroom and get ready for bed. As I leave the bathroom to head down the short hallway to my bedroom, Ben comes out of his room.

"Hey," he says to me, and I look at him over my shoulder. "I like your new hair." He smirks at me.

I murmur a quiet thanks, say goodnight, then hurry into my room and shut the door behind me. I lean against the door with a smile on my face. Those damn butterflies are swirling around in my belly again.

I fall asleep easily for the first time since moving into the apartment.

13
Emily

We get into a pleasant rhythm over the next week. Ben works as an engineer and has a standard nine-to-five job. He seems to be a bit of a workaholic, though. Since I still have about a few weeks left of training for my new job in the ICU, I've been stuck with the same hours as Ben. I never realized how exhausting it was to work five days a week instead of shift work.

One morning, as I get ready for work, I hear a knock at the door. My automatic reply is to tell them to come in but then realize that probably isn't appropriate for acquaintances, much less new roommates. Instead, I yell out that I'll be out in a minute.

Normally, I shower at the end of a grueling, back-breaking shift at the hospital, but since I've had this training, I've had to get ready in the morning. I walk out of the bathroom, and Ben is in the kitchen making breakfast.

"Good morning, the bathroom is free for you," I say to him as I head back into my room to get dressed.

I hear him get into the shower as I grab my work bag from the bedroom. I pass through the kitchen on the way out the front door to find that Ben left a note on the small table we bought for the apartment.

"Made some breakfast for you. Have a good day—Ben."

I can't help the smile that stretches across my face. This is the first breakfast he has ever made for me. To avoid the morning commute, I usually leave early for work and don't have time for breakfast.

I'm so touched by his unexpected and thoughtful gesture. Logan's never done anything remotely similar for me before. I'm giddy with excitement as I pack my work bag. Feeling like a schoolgirl whose crush has finally noticed her.

I grab the food he made for me, shoot him a text to thank him for breakfast and head out the door. I'm eager to start my day.

♥ ♥ ♥ ♥ ♥

After a grueling work week, I am exhausted. I can't wait for training to be over so I can get back to my three-day work weeks of twelve-hour shifts. Yes, the days are longer, but I have more days off to recover. I'm about to change into pajamas and call it a night, but I think better of it.

I text Ben and a few of our mutual friends to invite them to happy hour. Nearly everyone sends a reply that they want to go, except Ben.

I throw my phone on my bed and walk over to my closet to find an outfit for tonight when I hear the front door open. He must have been driving when I sent my message and probably hasn't seen it yet.

I walk out of my room to greet him and come to an abrupt stop as I almost run right into Ben, who is heading into his room.

"Oh, I didn't see you there," I say, my breath caught in my throat.

"Hey, roomie," he says in greeting.

"Did you see my text about happy hour?" I ask in a rush.

"Are you asking me out, roomie?" He smirks.

"Well… I mean, yeah, if you want to go. I invited some of our friends, too." His smile dims a little before he perks up again.

"Yeah, let me get changed first."

"Okay, I'll meet you in the living room, and we can walk down together."

"Sounds good," he says before moving around me in the narrow space. Our bodies don't touch, but I can still feel his body heat as he steps away.

I shiver and head back into my room to finish getting ready.

Ben's changed out of his button-up shirt, tie, and slacks and is now dressed in dark jeans and a fitted long-sleeved Henley. I normally dress for comfort over style, but tonight, I dressed up a little with a sweater dress, tights, and knee-high boots.

We're both appraisingly looking over the other person before bringing our eyes to meet. We smile at each other and head toward the front door.

I guess we're both excited to be single and ready to mingle.

Having someone to navigate this next stage together feels like a breath of fresh air.

♥ ♥ ♥ ♥ ♥

Ben and I are at a high-top table in the bar area as our friends slowly trickle in. I know the whole point of having a wingman is to find someone to take home for the night, but I'm having so much fun with my friends that I don't even bother looking around at the crowd of corporate males swarming the bar.

The music is loud, and it's hard to hear each other over the crowd, but I'm feeling relaxed and enjoying my glass of wine. Logan and I rarely ever went out. He adheres to a very strict diet, which does not include alcohol unless it's a special occasion. It's never bothered me before, but sitting here with my friends makes me realize that maybe there is a part of life that I have been missing.

I know that a lot of social events circle around food and alcohol, and because of those things, Logan and I opted to stay in instead to avoid temptation.

I must get lost in my thoughts because I startle when Ben leans over to whisper in my ear.

"What are you thinking about, roomie?" His voice is husky, and I feel a tingle spread through my body.

"N-nothing," I stammer and turn to face him. Our faces are inches apart. This close to him, I see he has hazel eyes brimmed with dark eyelashes that are enviable. He sports a neatly trimmed beard with dark hair spiked messily but artfully. I glance down at his lips just as he pokes the tip of his tongue out to lick his lower lip.

I bring my eyes back to his, and it's like we're the only two people in the bar as the room fades away. It feels as though the world has been spinning around me at a fast pace, and time slowed down in this moment.

Jason pushes Ben's shoulder and breaks us free from our stare-off.

"Did you hear what I said?" Jason asks Ben, and Ben just shakes his head in reply before turning to look at Jason. They're best friends from college, but they also work at the same company. I've heard stories of the two of them climbing the corporate ladder to land their high-ranking jobs that require a level of dedication to their job that I don't envy. Unfortunately, this means that they're often talking about work, even at happy hour.

I love that I don't have to take any of my work home with me when I'm done at the end of my shift. Other than the emotional and mental trauma of the day-to-day occurrences in a hospital setting, I rarely think about work when I'm off. I've used working out as my therapy to cope rather than seeking a professional therapist, though I guess I could probably benefit from having one of these days with recent events.

Since I have little to contribute to their conversation, I look around the bar. There seem to be a lot of attractive young guys out tonight, but most of them seem to be attached to equally attractive young women. It's hard to tell if any of them are single or if they're in relationships.

Amanda is savoring her ginger ale as if it were the best drink she's ever had. She keeps looking at my wine longingly. I know she misses wine, but she can have some soon after the baby arrives.

Her descriptions of her body's changes during her last month of pregnancy are making me cringe. "Have you two hooked up yet?" Amanda asks in a whisper, turning to me."

My eyes widen, surprised by her unexpected question.

"What? Of course not!" I hiss in reply.

Stifling a smile, Amanda surveys the crowd. With a nod of her chin, she directs my attention to a guy by the wall. "You should go after that guy. He looks single and ready to mingle."

My jaw drops in surprise. Amanda is aware of my lack of one-night stand experience. I had zero interest in casual sex before.

"You should do it. Let me know what it's like to be single again," she whines, though I know she's just being silly.

I smile, a wry shake of my head accompanying the silent laughter building within me. I don't even glance at the person she was pointing to. This isn't the right time or place, and I'm having too much fun to bother.

"See anyone you like?" Ben whispers in my ear again. God, why does he keep doing that? It's like he can't resist startling me.

"Umm… no, not really." I tuck my hair behind my ear.

"Good," he replies. He seems relieved by my answer.

After finishing another round of drinks and appetizers, I yawn and look over at Ben, who is still in a deep conversation with Jason, who's gesticulating wildly. Jason has always had a loud personality, but he really gets excitable and shockingly louder when he's had a few drinks.

As if he senses my gaze, Ben looks over at me and tips his head toward the door as if to say, "Are you ready to get out of here?"

I nod enthusiastically and put on my coat. I throw some cash on the table to take care of my portion of the bill and walk up to Ben and Jason as they're saying their goodbyes.

"Ready to go, roomie?" Ben asks, and I nod as we make our way out of the restaurant.

Once outside, the cold winter air feels refreshing compared to the warm and crowded bar. The short walk back is mostly in silence, and I'm thankful. I've never been much for small talk, and Ben seems to be the same.

Once we get to our apartment, he takes out his keys and lets us in. He lets me use the bathroom first to get ready for bed. As I leave the bathroom, I stop short again as Ben is right outside the door.

His cologne smells delicious.

"Oh, um, I'm done..." I look up at him. He's staring at me intensely, his pupils dilated as he peers down at me. His hand moves up as if to brush the hair out of my face before he lets it drop back down to his side in realization of what he was about to do.

He backs up a step so I can move past him, and I scurry into my room. I shut the door quietly behind me and lean up against the door with my heart hammering in my chest.

What just happened?

14

Emily

Valentine's Day has never been that important to me. Of course, when you're in a long-term relationship, it's considered an important holiday. Everyone my age is engaged or married, with one-and-a-half kids on the way. Yet, here I am, almost thirty years old and back on the market. When you're single at my age, Valentine's Day is like a mark of shame on your character. The red glowing scarlet letter that signifies your single status.

Even when Logan and I were together, he always seemed to forget that most boyfriends mark the holiday by showering their ladies with gifts or signs of affection. I always told myself that I didn't need any presents or flowers to know that he cared about me, though I always felt a pang of disappointment every time he forgot. I comforted myself by knowing that he loved me and that we were end-game, so what does it matter in the long run?

The dreaded Hallmark holiday is fast approaching. Thankfully, I have a long shift at the hospital scheduled. My classroom training is almost over, and now we're at the clinical portion of the program where I shadow my mentor as they go about their workday.

It is much more invigorating to be back on the hospital floor than it has been sitting in a classroom for the past few weeks. I'm excited about moving on to the next part of my training.

I've always known that I wanted to be a nurse. My grandmother, who was a Vietnamese refugee and my idol, had type 2 diabetes and would often need help to take care of giving her insulin doses. Not only would she ask me to help her, but she also had me helping with cupping, an Eastern medicine therapy involving the use of special cups to create suction on a person's body that was believed to help draw out the toxins in the body.

I've always felt honored that she picked me out of all of my cousins to help her. Granted, my cousins and even my siblings were wild and rambunctious. They probably wouldn't be very calming to be around during a cupping session.

I always thought that I would end up working in the neonatal ICU. Instead, my new job is in a Level 1 surgical trauma ICU. I found that after shadowing a NICU nurse, I couldn't handle the stress of holding somebody's child's life in my hands. It's funny where life leads us sometimes.

It's almost time for a lunch break when I hear my name being paged overhead. I find my manager, who informs me that security has called for me to come downstairs to the lobby. I do not know what it's about, but head out of the secured unit and down the bank of elevators to the lobby.

I walk up to security and tell them I was called down here by my manager. The security guard looks at my work badge to verify my name and tells me he'll be right back. He disappears into the office and comes out carrying a giant vase of red roses with a stuffed puppy attached to the bottom. I step aside, thinking he is handing it to someone else when he stops in front of me. He places the vase down and hands me a clipboard and a pen.

"Sign here that you got your delivery, please."

I look up at him, confused, but do as he says. I hand over the clipboard, and he puts it away and hands me the vase. Did

Logan send me flowers? This seems so unlike him. I hadn't really heard from him since he found out I was living with Ben.

I'm walking away with a giant vase in my hands and don't stop to look at the attached card until I'm back on my unit. My stomach is in knots. I'm setting it on the table in our shared break room when my best friend, Maggie, walks in. She sees the flowers and gasps excitedly.

"Did someone send you flowers on Valentine's Day?" she all but shrieks.

"Um…yeah, I guess so."

"Who are they from? Do you have a secret admirer?" Her excitement is palpable. She frowns. "Are they from Logan?"

I finally pull out the small card that's sticking out of the bouquet. My confusion must be obvious because someone suddenly yanks the card away. I look up to find Maggie reading the card, and she looks up at me.

"Happy Valentine's Day, roomie ;)" is what the card reads. I'm in shock as I try to make sense of the fact that Ben took the time to send me flowers on Valentine's Day when my ex-boyfriend never once took the time to even acknowledge the holiday.

"Oh my god. Are you guys hooking up?" Her eyes widen in surprise.

"What? No, of course not!"

"Then why is he sending you flowers on Valentine's Day if you're not hooking up?" she asks, which is a valid question.

"I don't know. We've never even talked about today before."

"Well, if you're not hooking up, you should." She winks at me as she bends down to smell the roses.

"I can't do that. We live together."

"Who says you can't? Besides, that's probably the best setup. You're both in the same apartment, sleeping just across the hall from each other. One of you sneaks into the other's bed and gets freaky. You know what I mean?" I think she's swooning now.

I'm laughing at her ridiculous behavior, and she looks at me with her big doe eyes.

"Wouldn't that be so romantic if you guys end up falling in love and getting married? After what Logan put you through, you deserve your happily ever after." She looks like she's about to cry.

"Okay, calm down. Nobody is hooking up with anybody, and we will not end up falling in love or getting married. We're just roommates."

"We'll see about that," Maggie states with a smirk.

I roll my eyes at Maggie. We met on our first day of orientation. We sat next to each other, unaware that they had hired us both for the same medical-surgical unit, along with two other girls. Although the four of us completed our training together, Maggie and I bonded over the shared trauma of being assigned evening shifts as new nurses.

Unfortunately, we both got to experience firsthand what it means when "nurses eat their young." We were being heavily bullied by the older nurses on the unit while we were on probation. Since we couldn't exactly report that we were being bullied by our superiors, being on probation meant that they could fire us for no reason. We suffered in silence while staying well past our shift to finish our documentation. We shared late-night snacks and listened to the soulful voice of Bruno Mars to help ease our pain.

We agreed to stick together for at least six months before quitting and finding a new job. Six months turned into one year, and now we're three years out, a little wiser but a lot more traumatized. She left to work in the ICU first. I stuck around for another year on our medical-surgical unit before finally working up the courage to follow her here.

It's been so nice to know that I have a friendly face among all the unfamiliar faces on the unit. I also know that she always has my back if I ever need it. So far, she's had nothing but kind things to say about our coworkers, and I'm excited about working in a healthy environment for the first time in years.

Before clocking back into work, I open my message thread with Ben and send him a quick message.

"Hey, did you send me flowers?"

"Who else calls you roomie?"

I smile because he's clearly the only one.

"Thank you. That was really thoughtful of you."

"No problem. I hope it brought a smile to your face."

I put my phone away. My heart feels light, and there are about a hundred butterflies taking flight in my belly.

I haven't felt like this in a while, if ever.

The further away I get from New Year's Eve, the better I feel, and I hope it continues to get better.

15
Emily

I'm woken up from sleep by the sunlight streaming into my bedroom. After a long twelve-hour shift at the hospital yesterday, I came home, showered, and went straight to bed. Ben wasn't at the apartment when I got back, and the lights were off when I went to bed.

I crack my eyes open and rub the sleep from my eyes. I hear him in the kitchen, so he must be cooking up breakfast or something. He has some soft music going, but I can't tell what's playing.

I stretch my aching muscles and roll over to get out of bed. Buffy and Spike are both asleep, still in the middle of my bed. I must have curled myself around their love nest in my sleep. They don't even flinch, their eyes still closed, as I rise and quietly open the bedroom door to leave.

After taking care of business and washing myself up to look semi-human, I walk into our kitchen. The aromas of pancakes, eggs, and bacon fill the apartment and make my mouth water. I need coffee before I can think about eating food. We only have a Keurig machine, but it seems I'm the only one that drinks coffee.

"Good morning." I say to Ben, who has his back turned to

me. He's wearing a white T-shirt and grey sweatpants. When he hears me, he turns his head to look at me over his shoulder.

"Morning, sleepyhead. I made breakfast if you're hungry."

"Oh, thank you. You didn't have to do that."

He gestures for me to have a seat at the table as he makes me a plate. Ben has already set the table with silverware. He hands me my plate and goes back to make himself a plate of food.

We sit across from each other as we dig into our food. After a few moments, he looks up at me.

"What do you have planned for the rest of your day?"

"Not much. I was just going to finish unpacking more of my things. What about you?"

"Same." He pauses before continuing, "Do you want to get dinner later at the new Italian place on Main Street?"

"Oh, sure, we can do that. Do you know if we need reservations?"

"I'll take care of it," he says as we finish up our breakfast in silence.

I've always found silence to be comforting and never felt the need to fill it with mindless chatter. I never noticed that Logan would often break the silence with conversation, as if the silence made him uncomfortable.

Ben seems to be not only comfortable but also at ease with the lack of conversation. As I'm getting up to clear my plate, our legs accidentally brush each other. I must imagine the electric charge that passes between us at the casual touch since I don't see him react other than to move his leg out of my way.

ও ও ও ও ও

I'm almost done getting ready for dinner when I hear music playing in the living room. I put some lip gloss on and roll my lips together before pursing my lips in the mirror and blowing myself a kiss. The red dress compliments my tanned complexion.

Since breakfast, I've gotten a good amount of unpacking and organizing done. I even left to go shopping at the local mall for some decor for the apartment and grabbed some lunch while I was out exploring the area. When I got back, Ben was in the shower. He texted me while I was out to let me know he had made dinner reservations for 6 P.M. That gave me enough time to lie down for a quick nap before I would need to get up and get ready.

It's about 5:30 P.M., and after giving myself a last glance in the mirror, I walk out to the living room to find Ben seated on the couch with a bottle of wine and two glasses already poured on the table. He's fiddling on his phone when he notices my approach. I almost laugh at his double-take as he takes in my outfit.

"Hey, I poured you a glass of wine. I figured we could share a drink before we head to dinner."

"I'd love that. Thank you." I sit across from him on the loveseat. Spike is sleeping on the back of the loveseat, and I give him a little pet across his head. The cats seemed to have acclimated much faster than I expected. I'm glad to see that he's happy and content with the new living arrangements.

Ben has some music playing softly in the background. I grab the glass of wine as he hands it over to me, and we settle in.

"You look nice." I feel heat spreading from my neck at the unexpected compliment and thank him.

We get to talking about our day and move on to other topics. The conversation seems to flow easily and doesn't feel forced. I've never felt so at ease talking to someone before. Ben has a natural ability to make me feel comfortable and not think too hard about what I'm saying.

"Oh, shit!" Ben exclaims as he looks at his watch. "It looks like we missed our dinner reservations."

Surprised, I look at my phone to find that we had been sitting there for almost an hour, just talking and enjoying our glass of wine together.

"Do you still want to go to the restaurant? I don't know if they will still seat us," I ask him.

"We can try another night if you want to just order delivery. Want to try that Chinese place everyone keeps recommending to us?" The Chinese restaurant in town is notorious for its weekend karaoke nights and authentic Chinese food.

"Yeah, that sounds like a great plan, actually."

I pull up the menu to the restaurant and tell Ben my order so he can call to have it delivered. We resume our conversation as we wait for our food to get here. The doorbell rings about thirty minutes later, and Ben gets up to get the food for us. I hear him thank the delivery guy and make his way back up the stairs.

He sets the bag of food on the coffee table, and I unpack the containers and utensils and set them out. I end up moving to sit next to him on the couch so we are both facing the giant flat-screen TV together. We scroll around for something to watch and eventually settle on the latest Marvel movie.

We sit in comfortable silence and eat our dinner. As the movie picks up, I can't help but sneak a few glances at him from the corner of my eye.

I've always found Ben to be attractive. He's tall, about six feet, and he's toned and fit without being too bulky. He has always had a clean-shaven beard for as long as I've known him. I've never been into bearded men before, but Ben wears it well. What I've always noticed about Ben from the beginning, besides his good looks, is that he's always smiling. His brilliant smile and charisma are dazzling to me. He's always appeared genuine in his interactions with anyone he talks to. But outside of large group events, we've rarely talked one-on-one before moving in together. That and the fact that his ex-girlfriend would give anyone with boobs dirty looks if they dared to approach him.

During the movie, we drift closer together so that our shoulders are touching. Sitting so close to him, I can smell the musk of his cologne. It smells like sandalwood with hints of vanilla. I'm tempted to lay my head on his shoulder, but I resist, if only because he'd probably think it's weird.

I internally roll my eyes at myself for the ridiculous urge. Despite living together, we barely know each other.

I guess all that wine is getting to me, and I feel my eyes getting heavy. I feel a sense of warmth and belonging as I drift off into sleep.

16
Emily

I'm startled awake when Spike jumps onto my shoulder and purrs. He sticks his whiskered nose in my face, and I realize three things at once.

One, I'm not in my bed. I must have fallen asleep on the couch during the movie last night. And, two, there's a warm body snuggled behind me. I know without looking that it's Ben. He has his leg tucked between both of mine as if it were my body pillow. At some point last night, we must have fallen asleep together, and I ended up being the little spoon to his big spoon. I vaguely remember him getting comfortable behind me, but I was too sleepy to realize what was happening.

The last thing I notice is that Ben is definitely sporting an impressive morning wood. My eyes widen at our predicament.

I push Spike off of my shoulder, who grumbles in protest, and slowly try to get out from under Ben's arm wrapped around my waist. It takes a few moments, but I'm finally free and sneak away to the bathroom. I risk a glance over my shoulder to find he's still sleeping before I disappear around the corner. The blanket he had wrapped around us is halfway on the floor, but I don't dare fix it in case he wakes up.

I shut myself in the bathroom and let out a sigh. I take care of business, flush the toilet, and brush my teeth. It's an early Sunday morning, so I still have time to climb back into bed for a couple of hours of sleep. I pulled on my dress, its fabric crumpled and stiff from a night spent twisted around me. I fumble with the zipper and tug the garment off of me. I rip off my bra and toss it into the hamper. Grabbing an oversized shirt, I tug it on over my head and sigh in relief as the soft cotton caresses my body.

As I'm crawling into my bed, I can't help but think about how well our bodies seem to fit together. I miss his warmth as I burrow into my cold blankets. Before long, I've fallen asleep again to thoughts of Ben and his mesmerizing hazel eyes and brilliant smile.

If only we weren't roommates.

17

Ben

I wake up alone on the couch. Well, I guess that's not entirely true. Buffy has curled her tiny body on the couch by my hips. Buffy must have taken Emily's place when she left this morning while I was pretending to still be asleep as she made her escape. She left behind her lingering scent of jasmine and vanilla in her wake.

Emily fell asleep on my shoulder last night when we were about halfway through Captain America: The Winter Soldier. It's not the most exciting of all the Marvel movies, so I don't blame Emily for falling asleep. I didn't have it in me to move her off of me, so I tried to lay her down on the couch. I grabbed the blanket and covered our bodies with it, creating a cocoon of warmth.

I try not to examine how I ended up just holding her against my body as I watched the rest of the movie. When the movie was over, I shut off the TV and just lay there with her in my arms. I must have fallen asleep because the next thing I knew, I woke up to Emily trying to make a quiet escape.

I've always had a tough time connecting with people, but Emily makes it seem so easy. Hell, I was with Melissa for nearly a decade, and we never knew what the other was thinking. She expected me to always read her mind and would get angry or upset at me when I couldn't. Unfortunately, we spent most of our relationship fighting. I should have left her years ago, but I stayed out of sheer stubbornness and a false sense of loyalty. I felt I owed it to her to make our relationship work. It wasn't easy walking away from my failed relationship, but we didn't make each other happy. Maybe we were happy together at one point, but that was so long ago that I can't even remember what it was like.

Emily, however, was like an open book. I could read her thoughts on her expressive face, though she likes to think she's good at hiding her emotions. I love that she says what's on her mind instead of hiding her true feelings. In our short time together, we've had simple conversations and even debated current events.

She scratches the part of my brain that craves intellectual stimulation. When Melissa and I were together, we mostly talked about work since we work for the same company and the latest gossip. I ended up tuning her out most of the time, which would always result in another fight.

Stretching, I finally get up and make my way to the bathroom. Emily's bedroom door is closed. I would love nothing more than to climb into her bed, pull her close to me, and have her tangle her legs within mine again.

But who am I kidding? We both just got out of long-term relationships. Neither of us is ready to jump into another one.

When I finally broke things off with Melissa, I knew I was done with relationships for a while. I was an idiot to think that proposing to Melissa would magically fix all our problems. If anything, it seemed to amplify our stark differences.

After finally admitting to myself that our relationship was over, I made a call to Jason, who had seen it coming from miles away. He let me move into his house while I figured out the next step. That was months ago, and I ended up staying with Jason and Amanda far longer than I expected. Work got busy, and I got used to having my best friend around. It helped ease the sting of my failed relationship.

When Emily approached me at Sasha's birthday party, I was shocked at first. I've always noticed Emily whenever she came around but never had time to get to know her. Melissa always seemed to hate her, so I attempted to avoid any one-on-one interaction with Emily. I barely gave it much thought when Emily asked me to be her roommate. It solved both of our problems. Plus, I could tell that Amanda was ready for me to get out of their space so that they could start baby preparations.

I thought it would be easy to keep things strictly platonic, but I'm finding that the more time we spend together, the harder it is for me to resist the urge to kiss her.

Sending her Valentine's Day flowers was probably a mistake, but I didn't want her to feel alone. I do not know what her douchebag ex-boyfriend did for the holiday, but her reaction to the flowers makes me think he didn't bother to do anything at all. I'm so angry about how Logan treated Emily that I'm considering committing a felony. Just once, I'd like to punch that smug bastard.

I make my way to my bedroom and turn around to shut my door, which faces Emily's door. After one last glance at her bedroom door, I finally shut mine and climb into bed.

Guess we're both in for a lazy Sunday.

18
Emily

The rest of the week goes by in a blur. I've been avoiding being alone with Ben, which really isn't that difficult considering I'm putting in long hours at the hospital. On my days off, I spend the morning resting and then going to the gym before running errands. I found a gym closer to my apartment. It was a hard transition at first, but everyone has been really welcoming.

When I get back to the apartment, Ben is usually at work, so I have the apartment to myself. I've been catching up on my reading lately. I had forgotten how much I loved to read, but I'm trying to find time for the things that I let go of when I was with Logan without even realizing it. If nothing else, this breakup has helped me to see all the things I changed about myself to be the perfect girlfriend for Logan.

It didn't happen overnight. I didn't wake up one morning and decide that since Logan didn't like to read, neither did I. Or that instead of disagreeing with anything Logan said, I would nod silently to avoid embarrassing him in social situations or appearing argumentative. I didn't want to be the girlfriend whom everyone pretended to be nice to only to become the subject of the cop wives' gossip behind my back. Having been

101

privy to some of the silly gossip, I had decided to never give them anything to talk about.

In the weeks since Logan ended things, I realized how much of myself I let go of to fit the mold of his perfect partner. I justified it, thinking we were endgame and would eventually be married. Besides, it wasn't like Logan was asking me to change myself.

So, I've been trying to recover pieces of myself that I lost. One of which is reading for fun. I love to read all genres, but romance novels make me the happiest. I love the stories of two people coming together and working out their differences to make a relationship work. The guaranteed happily ever afters are always an endorphin rush that both my heart and soul need. Romance books also help me feel less alone. How can you be alone when you have a plethora of book boyfriends?

Before what I've been referring to as "the couch incident," I would curl up on the couch with a book, my blanket, and a cup of coffee. But, ever since "the couch incident," I've relegated myself to holing up in my bedroom. I found a cute but trendy reading chair that fits perfectly in the corner of my bedroom. It also doubles as a place where I dump my clean laundry, but it works.

I'm not purposely avoiding Ben, but knowing that I may be catching feelings for my handsome roommate has been wreaking havoc on my nerves. My guilty conscience whispers that it's way too soon while the devil on my shoulder is telling me I should go for it.

It hasn't even been two months since Logan and I broke up, but it feels like a lifetime has passed. I feel like a new person these days. It makes me feel guilty that I'm not still in mourning about our failed relationship. It reminds me of that *Sex and the City* episode where Charlotte said, "It takes half the total time you went out with someone to get over them."

So, if that is "the break-up rule," according to the wise and

---

graceful Charlotte York, wouldn't that mean that I had to spend the next one and a half years getting over Logan?

What does it say about me when I have spent most of the time…not thinking about Logan? Sure, I've thought about him in the general sense. I've wondered how he was doing. And, yes, I've been trying to figure out how I was so stupid and missed all the signs that he had been unhappy for so long, but outside of that, I haven't missed him as much as I imagined I should.

Even worse, how do I tackle the thoughts that I've been obsessing over Ben since Sasha's party? Or that I seem to be almost hyper-aware of his presence in every room we're in. Or that I seem to harbor some insidious butterflies that take flight every time he smiles at me.

It seems awfully too soon to be thinking about a new guy right after a breakup. Though I can't even remember the last time Logan and I had sex. It had to have been before Halloween. I thought it was a normal rut that all couples went through and that we would eventually get back into the swing of things. When we first slept together, the sex was electric, which lasted for a few months, and we kind of fell into a routine. Logan liked the missionary position, which was fine. He used to get me off in the beginning, but I can't recall the last time I had an orgasm with Logan.

Most of the time, he would come, and as he was cleaning himself up in the bathroom, I would get myself off with my hands. Lately, I've been doing a lot of self-care to thoughts of a certain hazel-eyed roommate.

It doesn't escape me that we still haven't acted as each other's wingman or brought other people back to our apartment to hook up. Maybe that's what we need to do to help ease some of the tension between us.

19
Emily

B en and I are back at Billy's for happy hour. We're in the corner of the bar, each with a drink. We're mostly people-watching for the time being. After my epiphany, I texted him and asked if he wanted to go out. He didn't respond immediately, which made me question my decisions, but eventually, he texted me back, saying that he was leaving work and he'd see me soon.

It didn't take me long to get ready, but I dressed in my usual jeans and oversized sweater tonight. I was determined to try out this wingman/wingwoman thing and get each other laid. We needed this to happen so we could both move on from our past... right?

Ben got back to the apartment and greeted me from the hallway. I heard him go to his bedroom and assumed he was freshening up. When he emerged from his bedroom, he was in jeans and another tight-fitting Henley. Did he own anything else in that closet of his?

We were walking to the bar when I broached the topic of being his wingwoman for the night. He said nothing at first. But after a tense minute, he gave a curt nod.

"Sure, roomie. You can be my wingwoman tonight," he murmured softly.

That's how we find ourselves with our backs against the wall, standing close together but with about a foot of distance between us. We've been watching the crowd for maybe a half hour in silence, both of us sipping on our drinks.

I can't tell if he is upset or not, but he seems more tense than usual. His jaw flexes after every swallow of his beer, and I tried to ask him if he saw anyone he'd like to take back to the apartment, but he didn't even respond to me.

I finish my drink and turn to ask him if he wants another beer, but he shakes his head before I finish my sentence. Shrugging, I walk away from Ben and take a seat at the bar. The music is loud tonight, and the bartender has been steadily fixing cocktails and serving beer. He looks to be in his mid-thirties with a stylish coif to his dark blond hair. He's wearing his button-up shirt and vest uniform, with his sleeves rolled up to his elbows. I can tell by the way he moves that he's athletic. His brawny muscles flex as he whips up cocktail after cocktail. He was the same bartender from the first night Ben and I came here, so he recognized us when we walked in. As he walks over to me, I spy his name tag, which states his name is Scott.

Scott stops in front of me with his arms gripping his side of the bar.

"What can I get ya?" he asks in a friendly tone.

"What do you recommend I try this time?" Scott recommends I try the seasonal Moscow mule on the menu. Since I'm not much of a drinker, and I can't decide what I want, I'm thankful for his input.

Scott looks me over slowly before giving me a lopsided grin. I know he's flirting with me, but I know that it's part of his job. It still feels nice to be on the receiving end of male attention. It's almost like I perk up at his appraisal.

"How about something different?" he purrs and leans in a little closer to me.

106

I wiggle in my seat uncomfortably.

"Um, sure, I'll try anything."

"Anything, huh?" He winks at me before walking off to make my drink. When he comes back, I sense a presence at my back. I'm about to put cash on the bar top to settle the bill when I see a hand smack a credit card down in front of me. I trail my gaze up the arm, but I already know who it is.

Ben is glowering at Scott with his jaw clenched tightly. I see the muscle flex before he opens his mouth.

"I got her drink. I'll take another IPA."

Scott nods at Ben with a knowing smirk before looking down at me and giving me a wink again. I feel Ben tense behind me and sit on the edge of my seat as we wait for Scott to return with Ben's IPA. Finally, Scott unceremoniously plops the beer in front of me and settles the tab.

I turn to face Ben and am about to slide out of my seat, but since Ben hasn't moved his arm, I'm caged between him and the bar. I look up at him and find he's already looking down at me. My breath gets stuck in my chest as I take him in at such a close distance. His hazel eyes are dark as he stares into my eyes. Our faces are just inches apart, and I see his nostrils flare. His jaw is still tight as we gaze at each other.

I feel like a gazelle stuck in the gaze of a lion, and I don't dare move a muscle for fear of him pouncing on me. It's like the room disappears, and all I can see and sense is Ben.

I'm startled when I hear Scott yell. He must have been trying to get our attention for a bit.

"Here's your check."

I take a deep breath and scoot back into my seat so Ben can reach past me to sign the check. His arm brushes me as he hands the check back to Scott, and it sends a thrill through my entire body. I feel my core clench at the slight contact, and my face flushes with embarrassment.

Ben takes a step back, and I make my escape, excusing myself to go to the bathroom.

I lock myself in the bathroom and lean against the door. My heart is racing, and I'm feeling hot and bothered. The brief encounter with Ben felt so intense. Was he mad that Scott was flirting with me? I mean, Scott flirts with everyone, not just me. I've seen him flash the same lopsided grin and wink to many of his female patrons. I know that I'm not special to him other than how well I'll tip him at the end of the night.

Fanning myself, I use the toilet and walk over to the sink to wash my hands. I'm tempted to splash my face with water to cool down, but I doubt my mascara would survive the waterboarding. Instead, I wet some paper towels and place them over my neck and chest to cool down.

Once my heart rate has calmed down and I've reapplied another layer of lip gloss, I square my shoulders and take a deep breath. I walk back into the bar, which seems to have gotten more crowded in the short time I was in the restroom. I find Ben by the bar, but he's not alone.

A beautiful blonde dressed to impress in her tight dress and kiss-me-red lips is talking animatedly with Ben. I watch as she leans in close to him and whispers something in his ear. Ben smirks at whatever she says, and he looks over her shoulder to find me standing awkwardly at the edge of the crowd.

It looks like he's about to get lucky, and even though I feel like my heart dropped out of my butt, I muster up an encouraging smile and a thumbs up. If I was alone, I could slap myself for making such a stupid gesture. I don't want him to think I'm upset with him for talking to another girl. Besides, that was the whole point of tonight, wasn't it? So we could help each other find someone, even if it's just for the night.

Even if that was the plan going in, I suddenly feel sick to my stomach and just want to go home. I work my way through the crowd to the front door, and when I step outside, the cold air is a stark reminder that I left my jacket at the bar. I hope Ben remembers to grab it on his way back with whoever he was talking to at the bar.

I've barely made it a block before I hear hurried footsteps behind me. I look over my shoulder, but before I can make sense of what's happening, I'm grabbed by my upper arm and pushed up against the building. Arms braced by my head, I look up to see it's Ben. His posture is tense with restraint. I gulp as I stare up into his eyes as they bore down into me. His pupils are huge and obliterate his beautiful hazel eyes. He's breathing through flared nostrils, and I see the muscles in his jaw tick with anger.

"Never leave like that again," he commands in a low growl.

My tongue is stuck to the roof of my mouth as I gape at him.

"Do you understand me?"

I nod in answer.

He edges closer, his eyes darting between mine; then, with a frustrated growl, he steps back. Running his hands through his hair, he turns away, hands on hips. He has my coat across his shoulder. He takes it and gestures for me to put it back on.

I'm bewildered as he helps me put my coat on. I'm not sure why he seems so agitated. I've never seen this side of him before.

"I'm... I'm sorry..." I stammer, though I'm not sure what I'm apologizing for.

He nods brusquely and gestures for me to lead the way back to our apartment. After a hesitant moment, I take a step and we begin our short trek back. We don't talk until we're rounding the block to our apartment.

"You left without me," he retorts.

"Oh. I thought... I thought you and that girl were..."

"You thought wrong."

My brows furrow in confusion, and I glance at him. He takes a deep breath and clenches his fists.

"She's friends with Melissa. She saw me at the bar and wanted to know what happened."

Oh. Well, I guess I read the situation completely wrong...

"I saw her whispering in your ear, so I thought... you know..."

"She wanted me to bring her back to our apartment."

"What?"

"I told her no."

"You told her no?" I question.

He nods in response.

"Why?"

"Because I don't want her." He says nothing else as we make our way into our apartment. He follows me up the stairs and helps me get my coat off once we're inside.

I turn to thank him, but the words get stuck in my throat. I see his hand reach up to curl a strand of my hair around his finger before tucking it gently behind my ear. I look up at him, and we stand there together. Taking each other in and breathing the same air. It always feels like the world stops turning when we're together like this.

We're interrupted by the angry yowling of two hungry cats. We break apart, and I hurry to get the cats their wet food. They have a constant stream of dry food available all day and night, but I like to give them wet food at least twice a day. They hate it when I'm late and are being very vocal about their displeasure. I can't help but smile at their antics, even if they broke up an intense moment with Ben.

Ben heads into his bedroom, and I sneak into the bathroom to get ready for bed. When I come out, I'm stopped short again by Ben standing just outside the door.

"Jesus!" I exclaim, placing a hand on my heart. "Why do you keep doing that?"

He says nothing but smiles down at me.

"Good night, roomie," he finally says. It sounds like a rumble when he talks this low. It does crazy things to those damn butter-flies in my tummy. I try not to clench my thighs at the sudden ache in my core. Seriously? A simple goodnight turns me on? I need to get laid or find a new vibrator.

"Um, goodnight!" I say in an all too high-pitched voice. Since he won't give me any space, I dodge him and rush into the safety of my room. I swear I hear him chuckle as I slam the door shut and lean against it.

I change into an oversized sweater and sleep shorts and climb into my bed. For a minute, I lay there feeling restless and needy. I slip my hands down my body and into the waistband of my underwear. Knowing he's just outside the door, I am too paranoid to find my vibrator in case he can hear through the thin walls, so my fingers will just have to do for now.

To be honest, I've been on edge all evening, and I'm already wet. Feeling a jolt of pleasure travel up to my core, I stifle a moan while rubbing my clit, making me even wetter. I glide my other hand down and insert it slowly into my core. I let out a gasp at the intrusion and thrust my finger while still keeping a steady pace, rubbing my clit. Needing more friction, I add a second finger.

Thoughts of Ben fill my mind as I pleasure myself, and I imagine things ending a little differently tonight. I remember the feeling of him pushing me up against the building earlier tonight, his arms on either side of my head, keeping me trapped, but this time, he grabs me by the throat and slams his mouth down into mine with a harsh and possessive kiss.

I pretend that he's so desperate to have me as he unbuttons my jeans, not caring that people could walk by at any moment, and fingers me against the building. I picture the way I grip his biceps, not in protest but in pleasure, as he plays with my clit with his thumb. And then, when he breaks the kiss, he looks at me with a devilish glint in his eyes and says one word.

"Come."

And I fall apart at his command.

I'm breathless and panting when I finally come down from my orgasm. That was probably the most intense orgasm I've had in a while, and my body feels relaxed as I drift off to sleep.

20

Ben

This is such a cluster fuck.

I watched Emily scurry into her room like a scared little mouse, and fuck if that didn't make me want to chase after her, pin her down, and have my way with her. She makes me feel like a caged lion just waiting to be let out so I can pounce on her and make a delicious meal out of her. I bet she'd love every second, too.

I don't know what she was thinking, running out of the bar like that earlier. Even if she thought I was going to be taking another woman back to the apartment, I never would have wanted her to walk back alone. The thought of anything happening to her makes my stomach curdle. As soon as I saw her leave the bar, I shoved Shannon out of my way to catch up to her, barely remembering to grab her coat as I was leaving. I hardly registered Shannon's shocked yelp as I rushed past her out the door.

Shannon did proposition me to bring her back to the apartment. While I'd always been cordial with Shannon, I never let her think I was ever interested in her while I was with Melissa.

Unfortunately, we both work for the same company, and the company sometimes assigns her to the same projects as me, so

I've tried to maintain a professional distance from her. She had come over when Emily had gone to the ladies' room and started yapping about work and her latest project. She told me that Melissa had told her we had broken up, but she acted like she didn't know what happened. Then she told me how she thought I was too good for Melissa and leaned in to ask me if I could take her back to my apartment and show her around. I knew what she was hoping for by her request.

I know women find me attractive, but I've always been a one-woman kind of guy. I was about to turn her down when I saw Emily, who grimaced at me and gave me a thumbs-up. She didn't even wait for me as she took off.

I was livid by the time I finally caught up to Emily. I wanted to do so much more to her than hold her against the building. The urge to bend her over and punish her for daring to leave without me was so strong. I felt like a live wire ready to explode at the smallest provocation. I didn't want to scare her, and I knew I was acting like a possessive ass, but damn, she drives me crazy.

I know what Emily thought was happening, and she wasn't wrong. But she didn't even give me a chance to explain before jumping to the wrong fucking conclusions. When Emily proposed that we be each other's wingman, I thought it was a brilliant plan. I wasn't looking for another serious relationship so soon after things with Melissa basically blew up in my face. If I were honest with myself, it was a bigger hit to my ego and pride that I couldn't seem to make her happy. It wasn't like I was still head over heels in love with Melissa anymore. We both mistakenly thought that getting married would somehow fix all our issues. That was one of the most expensive mistakes I've made to date.

I know little about what happened between Emily and her dumbass ex-boyfriend, but I knew she needed to let loose, too. So, yeah, hooking up with random women sounded like a great plan.

Unfortunately, the more time I spent around my new room-mate, the more I became bewitched by her. I watch her more often than I care to admit. What is it about her? I can't seem to keep my eyes off of her.

The walk back was tense while I battled to calm down the rage demon that had taken hold of me when Emily took off. I felt on edge. Like a scared kid, I ran to my bedroom to regain control. I could hear the bathroom sink turn on, assuming Emily was getting ready for bed.

I get changed and come out of my room. I'm a little calmer now, but the urge to break down the bathroom door and force myself into her space is still strong.

I know I startle her when she comes out of the bathroom, and I can't help the thrill it gives me to see her eyes widen in shock and maybe a bit of fear.

It makes my cock twitch as she runs into her room, thinking that a flimsy door would keep her safe from me. If I really wanted to, I could easily kick down her door, pin her to the bed with her ass up, and rip off her pants before she could say my name.

Fuck. Now my cock is rock hard.

I enter the bathroom and turn on the shower. Keeping the temperature cold so I can calm my racing thoughts and libido. I've never been this turned on by someone before. The kicker is that there's hardly been that much flirting on either side. I know she finds me attractive by her lingering stares when she thinks I'm not watching her, but she's never acted on the attraction before.

I'm turned on by everything about her. Her calm demeanor. Her soft and shy smiles when she's deep in thought. The way she cares for her patients. She has such a big heart, but I can tell that she's still hurting. If I ever see her stupid ex-boyfriend again, I'll choke the life out of him for how he treated Emily.

I knew there was something off about him. He came across as a real asshole to me at Jason and Amanda's parties. But it had been none of my business back then. What type of imbecile would kick his girlfriend out without a valid reason? What was the reason behind their split? Emily deserved a lot more than a cruel breakup and then being kicked out on the streets right after.

Yeah, if I ever ran into him again, I would definitely be in jail. Who cares if he's a fucking cop?

I get undressed and hop into the shower. I've had a raging hard-on that's been desperate for my attention since our encounter outside the bar. I don't want to beat off to illicit thoughts of my roommate, but remembering how her breath hitched as I had her pinned to the wall makes a drop of pre-cum leak out the tip of my cock.

Fuck, if her parted lips didn't make me want to shove my hard cock in it and give her a taste of what she does to me. The worst part is she has no clue about the effect she has on me. She has no clue that I've never been more excited about coming home to our apartment to now than with anyone before. She is ignorant of the fact that my body hums with awareness whenever she's around. I'm hyper-aware of every movement she makes and the sounds she makes around me. I don't even think she knows that every little thing about her turns me on to the point of insanity.

My cock is rigid now and begging for release. I cave and grip the base of my shaft, giving myself a few experimental strokes. I bite back a groan at the pleasurable sensations. The cold water does nothing to quell my desire for Emily, who is just on the other side of this wall. I place my hand on the cold tiles, pretending I could reach her through the wall. I picture her on her knees in front of me. Those kissable full lips parted as I run my cock across her mouth. I have a hand in her hair, pulling on it to tilt her face up so I can see her better. I imagine her face is wet from the cold shower, but I imagine the eagerness in her eyes to take my cock. After a couple more teasing strokes along her mouth, I command her to open her mouth and shove inside without preamble.

My strokes increase in speed at the escalating imagery of Emily sucking at my cock, struggling to deep throat it when I hit the back of her throat. After a few tries, she gets the hang of it, and I'm seated in the back of her throat. I let her struggle to take a deep breath for a few seconds before withdrawing and allowing her to breathe. It feels so real that I finally blow my load onto the shower walls with a strangled grunt.

I let my head sag as I catch my breath. I can't believe I actually jerked off to thoughts of Emily. There's no way this arrangement will be platonic for much longer, judging by the intensity of my orgasm.

I wash all evidence of my release down the drain before shutting it off and grabbing a fresh towel to dry off. Wrapping the towel around my waist, I head back into my room for the night.

Emily's bedroom door is shut, and I hope my bathroom activities reached Emily's ears.

I have a feeling that pretty soon, we won't be going into separate bedrooms anymore.

21

Emily

The following week moves at a glacial pace as I try to avoid being alone with Ben as much as possible. I know I'm being a coward, but how am I supposed to look him in the eyes again after I masturbated to thoughts of him the other night? Or that it wasn't the last time? I have been feeling restless and jittery, like my skin is being stretched too tightly. If Ben so much as brushed his finger accidentally against me, I swear I would implode with the pressure building up under my skin.

It hasn't been too hard to avoid him, at least. I guess it's the perk of working long shifts: early mornings and late nights, eat dinner, shower, sleep, then rinse and repeat. This time of year, it's dark when I head into work, and it's dark again when I get out. It makes for a depressing season, but the distraction has been necessary for my sanity's sake. When I'm not busy at work, my mind drifts to thoughts of Ben, and I wonder what he's doing or if he's thinking about me. Then, I berate myself for even thinking he would think about me.

By the time I get home, I'm usually so exhausted that it's a chore to even make myself dinner. Most of the time, I don't see him before it's time for me to go to bed. I think he works a lot of late hours and he seems to really enjoy his job. It's kind of refreshing to see someone enjoying their career. He seems motivated to climb the ladder to be the top executive of his company.

I usually hear him making his way into the apartment when I'm already climbing into bed. Even though he can't see me, I always tense up in anticipation. My skin buzzes as I strain my ears to listen to his movements. Unfortunately, it's like he's trained me to respond to his presence, and as soon as he's around, my core gets achy. The need to be filled and stretched is unbearable. I don't have any fancy dildos or toys, so my hands have been doing the job for me.

The orgasm is usually quick but feels empty. I wish things were different and that I could act on this impulse to jump him as soon as he got home and ride his cock until the emptiness was gone.

Ugh. I never once felt these urges when Logan and I were together. Sure, the sex was nice, but it was predictable. I have never felt this on edge before. I honestly don't know how much longer I can resist Ben before I combust.

These days, Logan has barely been on my mind. Nowhere near as much as I think about—or obsess is more like it—Ben.

Logan continues to text me, which is perplexing. Earlier in the month, he sent a message asking if the oven mitt I left behind was something I wanted and if he could drop it off for me. I declined his offer until the next time he found another random item I mistakenly left behind.

It's odd that he texts me so much, given how eager he was to get rid of me. I expected him to end contact with me after I moved. That's what things were like when we were broken up, but I was still living with him.

The more that time passes, the more clarity I get about the state of our relationship. It's a little too late to recognize that while we seemed compatible on paper, we severely lacked chemistry. There was sexual attraction initially, but Logan never made me feel like my skin was on fire just by being in the same room as him. He never made my core clench with desperation just by sitting close to him. The thought of being touched by him did not leave me breathless.

Ultimately, I am glad that Logan ended things, even if I wish he could have gone about it differently. Who knew how far I would have let things carry on if he hadn't ripped the wool from over my eyes?

While I was still battling with the feeling of guilt that I should take longer to "mourn" our relationship, I realized what really bothered me about the whole situation. The only part that seems to raise my blood pressure is the callous way Logan went about it.

I felt so disrespected. He didn't even have the decency to talk to me before he decided we were over. Would it have made a difference? Probably not, but isn't that the whole point of being in a relationship with someone? Talking to them about your feelings or doubts?

He never even clued me in on his thoughts because he never loved or respected me. That surely hurts my ego and my heart. This whole time, I thought he cared about me, and he was probably thinking how sad and pathetic I was to still be hanging on to him.

Logan. Is. The. Worst.

Heaving a dramatic sigh, I go about my routine for the day. It's Friday, and other than going to the gym and catching up on some errands, I have little else planned for the rest of the day. The stars have aligned and granted me the weekend off. I'm thankful for the reprieve, but I don't even have any plans for the weekend. While I don't mind not having plans, I feel like it would be a disaster to be left home alone with Ben all weekend without a buffer between us. Maybe we should try that new restaurant again and invite some friends with us so we don't end up alone?

Yeah, I think that's a good idea.

♡ ♡ ♡ ♡ ♡

Well, that was a bust.

Apparently, everybody is busy tonight except for Ben. I didn't want to be a coward and bail on Ben when I realized that none of our mutual friends could join in on dinner plans. Translation: nobody was available to stop me from making a complete fool of myself and jumping Ben's bones. I don't think I have ever felt so nervous about being alone with anyone before, and it is incredibly inconvenient that it is also my roommate. Our lease doesn't end for another year, and there is no way I am going to break the lease early unless things end badly between us.

Do I think things would end badly between us? Honestly, who knows anymore? I thought Logan and I were endgame, and look where that ended up. The bigger question is whether I'm willing to take the chance again with somebody new. Talking to people about Logan makes me realize how awful he treated me. I know that I never want to be in this position ever again.

So, that's how we find ourselves at the new Italian restaurant, Mama Mia's, on Main Street. We're seated in a corner booth of the bar, which gives us the illusion of privacy. I thought things would be awkward between us, but our conversation has been flowing with ease.

When we accidentally touch each other, we pull away quickly, as if we are being zapped by electricity. It feels nice to know that he's not as unaffected as he seems. We're just finishing our main course before the server returns with the dessert menu. I'm stuffed, but I could probably find some room for dessert.

Ben lets me look over the menu first, and we decide to share a dessert—a molten chocolate lava cake. The server takes the menu from us. I sit back in my seat as the silence stretches between us.

Ben taps his fingers on the table as if he's contemplating something. I watch the rhythmic motion and try not to drool at the thick veins of his hands and forearms.

"Can I ask you something?" Although his voice was low, I could still hear him above the noise of the crowd. I tilt my head and wait for him to continue. "Have you heard from Logan?"

My eyebrows shoot up in surprise.

"Ummm…he's been texting me randomly. It's kinda weird, honestly."

The server returns with our dessert and places it in the middle. He lays both spoons down. "Enjoy."

The cake's richness is overwhelming, and I fight back a moan of pleasure as the flavor explodes in my mouth. The warm, gooey cake paired with the cool, creamy ice cream sends shivers of pure delight down my spine. The delightful contrast of temperatures that tantalizes my taste buds.

We're taking the last bites of the cake when Ben puts his spoon down on the table and leans back. I'm determined not to let any of the cake go to waste, so I scoop the last little morsel into my mouth and look up.

I can't make out what he's thinking, but he seems contemplative as he sits there, eyes half hidden in shadows, though I can feel the weight of his stare on me.

I try to keep eye contact, but the intensity makes me blush. I'm trying to resist the urge to wiggle in my seat before I hear him clear his throat. I look up at him with an eyebrow raised, waiting for him to say something to break the tense silence.

"Do I make you nervous, roomie?" His voice comes out husky, and I have to strain my ears to hear him over the din of the bar crowd.

"Um… no…"

"Liar." He smirks at me. Then he gets a serious look on his face. "Do you miss him?"

I'm taken aback by his question. In all the time we've spent together, Logan has rarely ever come up in conversation, yet he's come up twice tonight. It's almost like I forget he ever existed when I'm with Ben. Being around Ben has a way of making me lose track of both time and reality.

"No. I don't miss him," I answer honestly.

He must sense the truth in my words because his tense shoulders relax.

"Good," he states. "Very good."

"Well... what about you?"

"What about me?" he queries.

"Do you...do you miss Melissa?"

Ben tilts his head as if assessing me before answering with a short and perfunctory "No."

"Oh."

It's quiet for a moment before he continues, "I don't miss her because I don't love her. I stopped being in love with her a long time ago. I stuck with her for so long because I thought it was the right thing to do."

"Oh. Right, that makes sense." Does it, though?

"We dragged our relationship out way longer than we should have. I will always regret that, but I don't regret where it's led me."

"And where's that?" I ask, curious.

"I'm here with you."

I feel a blush creeping up my neck. I hope I don't look as flushed as I feel. The server comes over with our check at that moment, and I reach to grab it, but Ben snatches it away before I can. He glares at me as he gives the server his card before walking away.

We sit in tense silence until the server returns with the check. Ben signs it jerkily, and I gather up my coat and put it on. The walk back to our apartment feels taut with tension. I'm afraid to say anything. I can't tell what mood Ben is in now, but I get the sense that we're both about to implode with the slightest provocation.

When we're back in the apartment, Ben helps me get out of

my coat. His hands on my shoulders feel hot, and my body feels heavy. I chalk it up to the glass of wine we had with dinner. Just as I'm about to turn away, Ben grabs my hand, and I turn around to face him. He backs me up against the wall, and my breath catches in my throat.

He leans his head down, his nose skimming my ear as he takes a deep breath. My heart is pounding as I feel his soft lips gently brush over my cheek before he pulls back slightly. I'm staring at his lips as he pokes his tongue out and licks his lips as if he's trying to take the taste of me into him. My eyes move up to meet his. He inhales deeply, his nostrils flaring and pupils dilating.

"Fuck it," he growls as his hand reaches up to grip the back of my head and tilts my face up to meet his. Our lips collide like two storm clouds, and I feel the thundering boom ricochet inside my chest. He kisses me like he's been dying for a taste of me. His tongue roughly parts my lips and delves into my mouth. I moan at the intrusion, a rush of pleasure shooting straight to my clit. My hands come up to grip his biceps as he explores my mouth. He tastes sweet with a touch of smokiness, like the molten chocolate lava cake mixed with his whiskey.

If the wall wasn't at my back, I have no doubts that my shaky knees would have collapsed, and I would be a puddle on the floor. Suddenly, he pulls away, and we're both breathing heavily as he rests his forehead against mine. His kiss softens, but the stiffness in his shoulders and the barely perceptible tremor in his hands reveal the fierce restraint he struggles to maintain. My hands make their way up into his dark, soft hair as we continue to kiss like our lives depend on it.

When he pulls away next, he has a question in his eyes, as if to ask me if I'm okay with everything. He must see the answer he's looking for because he takes my hand and leads me back into our apartment. We say nothing as we head upstairs. He lets go of my hand so I can use the restroom, where I brush my teeth and wash my face with cold water to cool down my body temperature. Looking in the mirror, I see my face is flushed, my pupils are dilated, and my lips are swollen from the kiss. I raise my fingers to touch my lips gently as the warmth of butterflies fills my belly.

I take a deep breath and square my shoulders before opening the bathroom door. He's outside the door, already waiting for me, which seems to be a habit of his. He's watching me closely and gestures with his head to my bedroom.

Okay, looks like we're going to take this back to my room. He doesn't follow me right away as he heads into the bathroom, so I leave my bedroom door cracked for him. Part of me is anxious about picking up where we left off, while the other part of me is exhilarated to see that he feels the same way. I know we still have a lot to talk about, but we can deal with that later.

I go to my dresser and pick out a loose T-shirt and shorts. My boy shorts style underwear is kind of cute, at least if we take things that far tonight. Do I want things to go that far? It's probably too soon, but I've felt like I've been walking on eggshells around him lately, and I would love to release this tension between us.

I'm crawling into my bed when I hear the door creak open. I look up at Ben, leaning against the door jamb with his arms crossed. He watches me crawl onto the bed with hooded eyelids, and my body flushes when I realize he's likely imagining me on my hands and knees. I get under my bed sheets, and he makes his way over to me. He has changed into a pair of soft gray sweatpants and a basic white T-shirt, which looks amazing on his toned physique.

He sits down on my bed and settles against the back of my headboard. He looks down at me as he crosses his feet at his ankles. We stare at each other for a moment, neither of us wanting to break the spell.

Finally, as if afraid I would run away, he slowly reaches a hand to brush a lock of my hair out of my face. The gentle glide of his fingertips against my skin has my body vibrating all over again. I resist the urge to turn my face and nuzzle in his hand. Instead, I opt to watch the rapt attention he pays me. He retracts his hand and looks at me as if he's asking for permission.

I give a slow nod, and he gets under my duvet. He scoots himself down so that we're lying face to face, just inches apart but close enough that we're breathing the same air. Slowly, he leans forward and gives me a gentle kiss on the lips. He pulls back just enough so that he can whisper a soft goodnight.

I lay there with my eyes closed, just breathing in his scent. I can feel his body heat, and it makes me want to crawl into his space. I try not to second guess myself and move my body toward him. He opens his arms to me immediately, and I settle my head on his shoulder. He wraps his arms around me, and I feel like this is where I belong. With a final satisfying snap, the last puzzle piece fell into place, completing the picture and filling the void within me, bringing a sense of peace.

I fall asleep to the sound of his heartbeat. I know that when I wake up tomorrow, my life will never be the same.

22
Emily

I've never been much of a morning person. Normally, I have at least three alarms set and hit the snooze on my phone at least five times before my eyes even blink open. This morning, though, something is different.

It probably has to do with the warm body that's spooning me. Or that there is quite a large appendage that's stabbing my backside. With the feel of Ben's morning wood pressed against me, I clench my thighs tight and resist the urge to wiggle my ass against his crotch.

Sex should be the last thing on my mind, but I can't help but imagine Ben gliding his fingertips up the length of my thigh, causing goosebumps to erupt across my skin as he inches closer to my center. My clit is begging for attention, and I feel myself get wet as I imagine him reaching down the crease of my butt and pulling the crotch of both my shorts and panties aside as he discovers how wet I am from his ministrations. I pretend that he'll tease me with his fingers to get me ready for his giant cock, and then he'd take his cock out of his pants and…

"Morning, roomie," Ben's gravelly voice rumbles in my ear and startles me out of my daydream. Oh my god, can he see me blushing right now?

I clear my throat and look over my shoulder at him, giving him a small smile.

"Good morning!" I say, a little too shrilly. I clear my throat before asking, "How'd you sleep?"

"Best night's sleep in weeks." His smile is as radiant as the sunshine streaming into my bedroom window.

I roll over onto my back, careful to keep my distance because of morning breath and all. He doesn't move as I get comfortable and just watches me with his soulful eyes.

"I'm glad to hear that." I have to agree that last night was also one of the best nights of sleep I have had in a while. We say nothing for a moment before he brushes a strand of my hair out of my face. He seems to do that a lot, and I really enjoy it.

"Can I kiss you again?" he asks suddenly.

"Right now?" I squeak because, hello, morning breath!

"Yes, right now." His tone leaves no room for argument.

"Um, yes, but let me go brush my teeth first..." I make a move to get out of bed and am hauled back by a large arm. I'm flat on my back again, and his lips are on mine. I stiffen at first, but he coaxes my lips to take part. I can't resist him. Our tongues dance in a fight for dominance. My fingers weave into his hair, and I feel his hand pin me down by the hips as his upper body bears down on me. The weight of his body on me is delicious, and I feel a rush of arousal flood through my panties.

Who knew I could get so turned on by a kiss?

Pulling away from the kiss, I gasp for air, his breath warm on my skin as his soft, wet kisses trail down my jaw and neck. I turn my head to give him more access. He finds the sensitive spot where my neck meets my shoulders and bites down gently, causing me to gasp and buck my hips. He pulls back, and his eyes are full of amusement.

"Hmmm... you like that, don't you?"

I don't have time to respond before he slams his mouth back on top of mine. He repositions himself so he's between my legs, using his knees to prod mine open and make space for himself. I arch as his hips come into contact with mine and bend my knees so my hips cradle his. The movement makes me even more acutely aware of his cock. His very hard cock that I'm rubbing myself shamelessly against and panting with the friction it causes.

"Ohhh, god..." I'm moaning when he gives me a break from our kiss. My arms wrap around his shoulders as we grind our bodies together to mimic what it would feel like to have him inside me. With his forearm braced by my head, he reaches an arm down and raises my thigh, deepening the angle, and it drives me wild.

The sounds coming out of me are embarrassing but would probably make a porn star proud. I'm so wet as he continues to grind into me. He brings his lips back to my neck, peppering soft kisses along my collarbone, and then finds that spot again before softly licking it. He sucks on it gently, and then I feel his teeth clamp down on me. Before I know it, my core is spasming and clenching as I come hard. He doesn't let go of my neck or stop grinding until I've stopped screaming and thrashing around. Only then does he release my skin from his teeth, and I feel the gentle laps of his tongue as he smooths the bite.

His thrust becomes erratic, and then he groans and rests his head on my shoulder.

Did he just... Did he come in his pants?

We take a moment to catch our breath, and he rolls off of me to lie on his back, an arm covering his face like he's embarrassed.

"Fuck. That was..." He's still panting.

"Yeah, it was..." I look over at him, and he peeks at me from under his arm. I give him a shy smile, and he leans back over to give me a soft kiss on my lips.

"Let me clean up." His cheeks are flushed, and I look down to see the large, wet stains on the crotch of his sweatpants.

"Yeah, ok, umm... me too," I stammer as he rolls off and disappears down the hallway. I lay there for a second and catch my breath.

I cover my face with my hands and let out a soft groan. How did we even get here?

One minute, we're roommates, and the next, we're dry-humping like a couple of horny teenagers. Hell, I can honestly say that I was never involved in any type of awkward dry-humping before today.

My body heats at the memory of him coming from just the friction. Or did he come because he got me off? Either way, it's hot, and I'm in so much trouble.

I'm startled out of my self-deprecating moment.

"Hey," he says softly at the doorway, and I glance up at him. "I'm making us breakfast. Come out when you're ready."

I guess we're just going to pretend like this morning didn't happen? Maybe we can still be friends after this. Friends with benefits kind of deal. Or roommates with benefits would be more appropriate.

Yeah, I think if we work out the terms of our arrangement, neither of us will get hurt if things don't end well. Or if either of us finds someone else.

We both get what we want. No strings attached.

It sounds like a great plan.

23
Emily

I help set the table as Ben cooks fresh eggs and bacon with a side of buttered toast. He also had a cup of coffee brewing in the Keurig machine for me when I finally worked up the courage to face him. I gave myself a stern pep talk while washing up in the bathroom and changed into my least raggedy sweatpants and sweatshirt for the conversation. After all, I will not change myself for anyone. Not anymore.

I settle down at the table and patiently wait for him to join me. I'm catching up on the latest Kindle Unlimited borrow when Ben comes over with our breakfast. He places a plate before me and sits down. Mustering my courage, I look him directly in the eyes and sit up straight. Despite my little pep talk, I'm still nervous about how this morning will go. It doesn't help that I feel like he's staring straight into my soul and picking me apart from the inside.

Does he see what Logan saw? Does he think I'm not good enough for him?

I experience a fleeting moment of self-doubt. Dismissing Logan from my mind, I concentrate on the present moment.

"Thank you for cooking," I finally say, and he smirks at me before digging in. Ben doesn't drink coffee, which is so bizarre to me since it practically flows in my veins. Instead, he has a glass of fresh orange juice. I watch in rapt fascination at the way his biceps flex as he brings the glass to his full lips and how his Adam's apple bobs as he swallows.

I hear him chuckle and look up to see he's looking at me again in amusement. I swear I flush as red as a tomato. I pick up a piece of bacon and chew on it. After carefully swallowing, I wash it down with a swig of my freshly brewed coffee and burn my tongue.

After several tense moments, I break the silence.

"So… about earlier…"

"Yeah? What about it?" He has an eyebrow raised in question as he continues to eat his breakfast.

"I've never done anything like that before…" He smirks at me.

"Me neither."

"I know we both just got out of terrible relationships, so… I mean, it doesn't have to mean anything…" I trail off.

He suddenly tenses and puts his fork down gently on the table. He looks at me with a guarded expression.

"I don't want to, you know, make this a bigger deal than it is, and since we're both not ready to jump into a new relationship… maybe we keep things casual like a friends-with-benefits kinda thing? Only, well, we're roommates, so it would technically be roommates with benefits," I titter nervously.

Ben continues to look at me but says nothing for a moment before he dips his chin down in a nod.

"Roommates with benefits," he says slowly. "Sure, I can do that if that's what you want."

I let out a sigh of relief.

"Okay. Good. Perfect."

He clears his throat, and I look up at him.

"Let's get one thing straight."

My eyes widen at his serious tone, and I tilt my head in question.

"When you're with me, you won't be with any other guy. I don't share, and I don't plan on ever sharing you with anyone else. You got me?"

I nod in answer. I didn't even think about the logistics. Obviously, I wouldn't also be hooking up with other guys when I'm with him, but I guess he doesn't know that, so I'm glad he laid it all out on the table. But if I can't be with other people, then the rules should also apply to him.

"That sounds fair, but that also means you can't be with other women when we're together."

"Fine," he replies quickly.

"Okay, fine."

"Now that that's over, I'll give you a five-second head start."

"Wh-what?"

"Five."

My eyes widen in panic. He doesn't mean things start right now, does he?

"Four."

I bolt up and run into my bedroom, shutting the door behind me. I don't hear him finish his countdown, but within seconds, he's through the door and at my back, and my body temperature increases as I feel heat at my core.

"One," he says from behind me before placing a large hand on my shoulder and turning me around to face him. He cups my face and slowly brings his head down, and our lips meet in a gentle kiss at first. When he breaks the kiss, his hand moves to my waist.

"Let's try out this roommate with benefits thing."

"Right now?" I squeak out breathily.

"Right now," he states with finality.

"Okay." I gulp.

"Now, be a good roomie and sit on my face," he commands.

He backs us until his legs hit the edge of my bed. He sits down and looks at me expectantly.

"Um… can you close your eyes or something?" I ask

nervously. I've never stripped for a guy, and I'm anxious that he won't like what he sees. Even though I work out pretty consistently, I still have a soft belly that I'm insecure about. I've tried so hard to get rid of it, but it doesn't seem to want to budge.

His only answer is to scoot himself back onto my bed and lay back with his upper body braced on his forearms as he waits for me to undress. I take a deep breath and decide to just go for it and shuck my bottoms off but keep my panties and shirt on. He quirks a brow in question but doesn't protest.

"Crawl to me," he commands.

I place my hands on the bed on either side of his outstretched legs and make my way up his body. When we're face to face, he smirks at me as if to tell me to keep going.

Today seems like a day for a lot of first experiences for me. First, the dry humping, then the stripping, and next, am I going to really sit on his face?

I feel a hard smack against my butt, and I yelp in response.

"Hey!" I yell at him.

"I said, sit on my face, or did you not understand me the first time?" His voice is husky, and it sends shivers through my body.

"Jesus, you're so bossy," I mutter under my breath.

I slowly move up so that my knees are resting on both sides of his head. Knowing his face is so close and feeling his hot breath on me sends a rush of arousal to my center. I'm still wearing my panties, and I feel his large hands gently slide up the insides of my thighs. I swear I'm getting wet just from his touch. Then, he reaches up and kisses my crotch.

"Nice underwear, but they need to go." He helps me out of my underwear and tosses them over the side of the bed. He repositions me again, and this time, when I feel his hot breath, I can't contain the shiver that wracks through my entire body.

"Mmmm... You might want to hold onto the bed frame for this one."

That's the only warning I get before he brings my hips down to meet his hot mouth. I gasp as he starts with a soft kiss as if he's worshipping my pussy, and then I moan as his tongue parts my lips. He gives my entrance a gentle prod and licks his way up to my clit. He flicks at my clit with the tip of his wet tongue, and I grab onto the headboard with one hand, like he suggested.

I groan and try to move my hips to escape his onslaught, but his hands are holding me in place.

"Oh—oh my god." The sensations are intense, and I know I must be dripping wet. Ben switches it up and starts lapping up my wetness as it comes out of me. I use a hand to hold on to his hair and undulate my hips. At first, they're just small, unsure movements, but as the pleasure mounts, I'm grinding on his face shamelessly.

"That's it, baby. Ride my face." He sucks on my clit, and I let out a keening wail.

"Oh, fuck!" I'm pretty sure the neighbors can hear me screaming, and I don't even care. I feel the telltale tingle of an impending climax.

"Fuck. Fuck. Fuck. I'm gonna come!"

All I hear is Ben's growl in response before my body detonates in waves of pleasure. My body is shaking from the orgasm, and I have a fleeting thought that I must be suffocating Ben with my weight on his face.

He's giving me soft licks as he laps up the remnants of my orgasm, making me shudder. I collapse over him, my arms barely keeping my weight up when he picks me up and drags my body down until I'm face to face with him. He rolls us over so I'm laying on my back.

We're both breathing heavily, and he moves in to kiss me. I can taste myself on him, and I definitely made a mess of his face, judging by the wetness in his beard. The thought of tasting myself on him gets me hot again. I never realized how kinky I was, and I've never had an orgasm from oral sex before. It wasn't Logan's favorite, so he rarely ever went down on me, but man, can Ben eat a pussy. My pussy flutters in agreement.

His hand glides down to my pussy, still begging for his attention, and he slaps it. Hard.

I gasp in shock and resist the urge to squirm as a flood of heat rushes to my already-drenched center.

"Did I take care of this pussy?"

I nod gently.

"I need you to say it."

"Umm… you took care of my pussy…?" I squeak.

"This pussy is mine."

"What? No, it's not."

"Say it's mine, Emily," he demands, giving me a menacing glare.

I roll my eyes, and he smacks my pussy again.

"Ow! Hey! What was that for?"

"Don't roll your eyes at me unless you're ready for the consequences."

Oh my god, who knew that Ben was such a freak in the sheets? Not me. Nope. I had no clue.

"Now, try again. Tell me this pussy is mine."

"This pussy is… yours."

"Damn right, it is."

Ben pulls the duvet over me and gives me a kiss on the forehead. I'm about to reach for him and ask if he wants me to return the favor before he disappears into the bathroom. The next thing I know, I feel him crawling back into bed and pulling me close to his chest. I'm exhausted from multiple orgasms today. The last thing I remember before falling asleep is another soft kiss in my hair and his whispered words.

"Sweet dreams, roomie."

24
Ben

Roommates with benefits. She wants to be roommates with benefits. The idea made me scoff. I'm not against the mutually beneficial arrangement, but I'm mad that she thinks she can just walk away from me if she finds someone else. I'm not so egotistical as to think she couldn't find someone else, but she became mine the moment she put herself on my radar and asked me to live with her.

Recalling my last encounter with that arrogant prick still makes my blood boil. I wonder if Emily knows what a snake Logan really is. Even though Emily was off-limits to me back then, I saw Logan checking out other women whenever we were at the same parties. His blatant disrespect for Emily had made me irrationally angry. The regret of not fighting him then weighs heavily on my conscience. Now I'm even angrier at myself for not speaking up. Could I have prevented some of Emily's heart-break by talking to Jason or Amanda? It's too late now.

So, I'll be a good little boy and pretend that I'm cool with her plan. Meanwhile, I'll show her that the only person she'll ever need again is me. I won't let her go like that idiot ex-boyfriend of hers. The biggest mistake of his life is pushing Emily away. His loss is my gain.

I'm lying in Emily's bed with the taste of her cum still fresh on my tongue. I'm savoring her flavor like a decadent dessert. One taste won't ever be enough. I can tell by her hesitancy that she had never had her pussy eaten out like that before. I doubt she's ever come so hard either, judging by the way she tried to escape me when I felt her unraveling. The breathy moans and gasps of pleasure were the sweetest music I had ever heard. It makes me want to hear those sounds from her again. And the little hitch in her breath right before she warned me she was coming almost made me come in my pants. For the second time today.

I was so hard I had to run to the bathroom and fuck my fist. I emptied my balls into the toilet with her taste still fresh on my lips and her sweet sounds still singing in my ears. I washed my hands but don't bother washing my face. I wanted her taste to linger on my skin for a little while longer.

My libido is at an all-time high around Emily. It's almost like I'm a goddamned teenager all over again. I should probably question how this will all work out, but the only thing I care about is Emily. She's become such an integral part of my life in the short time we've been together. I can't help but be thankful for the circumstances that led us both to where we are today.

Sometimes, things need to fall apart so that better things can come together, even if it's the scariest shit in the world, like falling for your roommate. A roommate who you technically have only known for a few years, but know without a doubt that she has the heart and soul of a strong and kind woman.

Though we're only getting started, I can see our future together much more clearly. I know with absolute certainty that Emily is mine. Whether that means marriage and the whole kit and caboodle has yet to be determined.

I'm confident that the more time we spend together, the less guarded she'll be around me. That asshole really did a number on her confidence. I'll take it as slow as she needs me to, but I won't deny our attraction any longer.

Being with her intimately feels natural. Bringing her to screaming orgasms is my new favorite sport. Just like the running competition, I'm determined to win. She has no idea what she's in for. I'll make sure she feels cherished as I take care of all of her needs.

She'll never doubt her worth while she's with me.

25

Emily

"Can I please get a double chocolate cake with chocolate mousse to be ready for pickup this Saturday?" I listen as the woman recites my order and confirms the pickup time. I thank her, and we hang up.

I'm feeling a little frantic as I just learned that Ben's birthday is next week. After we woke up from our mid-morning nap the other day, we just lay in bed talking about anything and every-thing that came to mind. I felt so relaxed and comfortable around him. He made me laugh out loud with his sense of humor. He slyly announced he would turn thirty-five and was excited about his birthday this year.

He had turned to me and asked me if I was okay with him having a few friends over to celebrate this weekend, to which I enthusiastically agreed. It would be a combination of his birthday and a housewarming celebration, and since we have a lot of mutual friends, it would be nice to have everyone over. I thought it would also be the perfect opportunity to show off the apartment we've since decorated and turned into a cute and cozy living space.

Honestly, I never thought living here would make me so happy, but it feels amazing to be in my own space and not have to worry about someone kicking me out. The few weeks I spent thinking that I was going to be homeless were so stressful. I knew Logan only had so much patience with me before my time was up.

It feels like destiny had orchestrated this. The universe understood my deepest desires. Delivering what I needed in a cruelly beautiful package of heartbreak. I had to navigate through the sharp shards of the pain of losing everything I had built my life around in order to appreciate the opportunity that was granted to me.

I'd be lying if I didn't at least admit that it sucked at first. Like, really fucking sucked to have the rug pulled out from under me. I hated feeling off-kilter and lost. I don't know if I'll ever be able to forgive Logan for what he did. His texts continue to remain unanswered. I refuse to give him any more of my time.

So, that's how I ended up trying to plan for the best birthday/housewarming party ever. I found a fancy bakery that makes custom-order gourmet cakes. I know Ben isn't really into having the attention on him, so I figured that calling it a joint celebration would take the heat off him. Plus, who doesn't love chocolate cake? Even if said gourmet chocolate cake is going to cost a pretty penny, I'm sure that people will enjoy it.

I have a few more things to arrange for the party, like making sure we have enough food and snacks for everyone. We will probably need to get some alcohol, too. And, of course, we'll need some balloons!

I know it's just a party, but it feels important to make sure Ben has a good time. It's his first birthday as a single guy, though I never asked him what he normally did to celebrate. I'm sure Melissa threw him a birthday party or two, or maybe they're more of the "let's go out to dinner" for a private celebration kind of couple and then later take things into the bedroom…

No. I can't go down that path. I don't need to know every single detail of his relationship with Melissa. We're just having fun and enjoying each other's company—roommates with the extra benefit of multiple orgasms.

I flush at the memory of Ben commanding me to sit on his face like it's the most natural thing to tell someone to do. And then I get hot thinking about how amazing it felt to have someone be so selfless to bring them to orgasm and not expect it to be reciprocated. I mean, I would have reciprocated, of course. What guy doesn't want a blowjob as a 'thank you' for providing oral sex? I just assumed that was the natural way of things. He takes care of me, and then I take care of him.

Except, instead of expecting a blowjob, Ben disappeared for a few minutes. When he came back, I was already fast asleep. I should have felt embarrassed, but it felt nice not to have anything expected of me. That's the thing with being around Ben. I am always pleasantly shocked that he doesn't need or want anything from me other than my company. It's refreshing, and I didn't realize how long I'd been deprived of it.

That's why I want to make sure that this weekend is perfect for him. And not just for Ben, but for both of us. We both deserve a fresh start, so what better way than a party? Parties always bring in good vibes, and that's all I want for the next stage of my life.

Good vibes only.

♡ ♡ ♡ ♡

Saturday came faster than I expected, but I'm vibrating with excitement. It's the first time we're hosting a party, and I'm excited to play hostess with the mostest. I'd facepalm myself if my hands were free, but currently, I'm carrying in the super expensive gourmet double chocolate cake with chocolate mousse and whatever garnishments seventy dollars covers. The price tag shocked me, but I handed over my credit card with just a small wince.

I haven't told Ben about the cake, so I have to sneak it into the apartment and hide it in my bedroom closet, where some giant balloons are also hiding. When Ben was working yesterday, I got the balloons inside. I've been cleaning the apartment like a woman possessed all morning. As soon as I heard Ben leaving to go pick up alcohol for the party, I jumped in my car and drove the short distance to the bakery. It was only two minutes down the road, and I probably could have walked, but I didn't want to waste any time in case I couldn't get the cake inside before he got back.

I'm just about to put the cake in my closet when I hear the front door open and Ben yelling that he's home. He likes to let me know when he's back, and it always sends a shiver of anticipation down my spine.

For the past week, we've done our very best to keep our hands to ourselves. We usually fail at that within the hour of us being alone together.

The night always starts off innocently enough. We will be sitting on the couch with Netflix reruns of Friends, but I know neither of us is actually watching Ross' antics. We start with a respectable distance, but slowly, our bodies gravitate toward each other like two magnets that can't resist the other's pull. It's hard to tell who makes the first move or if we're so in sync that we move at the same time.

We clumsily make our way to my bedroom. Mostly, we have been able to keep our clothes on.

Okay, most of our clothes.

Well, okay, Ben usually can keep his clothes on, but I always seem to end up with no pants. It's like the man is a magician, and my pants just go poof!

Somehow, he has me writhing in pleasure from his hands, his mouth, or, if I'm really lucky, both his hands and his mouth as he brings me to a screaming orgasm every night. Honestly, I don't even know how he isn't bald by the amount of times I've pulled at his hair. But I have to admit that he looks good using my thighs as earmuffs.

I snicker to myself, and Spike gives me a questioning meow.

"I know, buddy. I am just hilarious, aren't I?" I swear Spike is judging me by his lack of response.

"Whatever. You love me anyway." He comes up and rubs his soft body against my legs.

"I take that as a resounding yes!" I reach down to pet his head, and his sister ambles over and demands affection. Lately, they have divided their attention between Ben and me. I swear I swoon every time I see him cradle Buffy in his arms or make room for Spike in our bed. I mean, my bed.

I shut the closet door and walk out into the kitchen to see Ben putting some beers in the fridge. His head peeks up when he hears me coming in, giving me a wide panty-melting grin with dimples and everything. My heart races as I stand there awkwardly.

"When is everyone coming over?" I finally break our stare off.

"I told everyone they could start dropping by around 5. You need help with anything else?" He gestures to the kitchen, which I have set up with snacks, plates, napkins, and plastic ware.

"Nope." I drag out the word, making the word pop. I put my hands in the back pockets of my jeans and rock back on my heels. "So… about tonight…"

He finishes putting the beers away and shuts the fridge door.

"What about tonight?"

"Do… Do your friends know? You know, about us?" I stammer unintelligently.

"No, I haven't told anyone yet."

"Oh." I deflate a little. I'm disappointed even though it's all very new for both of us. I can't help but think that maybe he's embarrassed about our situation.

"Do you want me to tell them?" he asks gently.

"What? Oh. No. No! That's not what I meant..." I rush to say, "I mean, I think we should just keep it between us for now. You know?"

"Like our dirty little secret?" He smirks at me now, and I can't help but blush.

"Yeah, it'll be our little secret." I smile at him and try to ignore the brief pang of disappointment that shoots through my heart.

♥ ♥ ♥ ♥ ♥

People trickle in and bring in their contagious cheerful mood. I'm greeting old friends and being introduced to a few of Ben's friends. The mood is uplifting, and I can't help but feel happy. It's been a while since I've felt this at peace, and I know part of it is because of my handsome roommate.

Ben is standing across the room with his back against the wall, one hand grasping a cold IPA and the other tucked into the front of his jeans pocket. He looks so at ease, but I know he keeps stealing glances at me when he thinks I'm not looking. I can feel the heat of his stare against the side of my face, but every time I look over at him, his gaze is never on me.

It feels like torture being in a crowd of people, and all I want to do is get him alone. Maybe tonight he'll let me take his pants off. I'd love to get a glimpse, and maybe a taste, of that impressive cock I know he's hiding from me.

"Emily, did you hear what I said?"

I'm shaken out of my reverie and realize that I must have zoned off with my dirty fantasies. I'm on the couch with Amanda, who is about ready to pop. She is expecting her first child any day now, and I couldn't be more excited for her.

"I'm sorry. What did you say? It's loud in here," I finally

answer her, clearing my throat and taking a small sip of my glass of pinot noir.

"I was just saying that I like the name Alexander or Joseph for baby names. What do you think?"

"I love both names, or you could call him Alexander Joseph and AJ for short?"

"Hmm… I actually kind of like that. Where's Jason?" Amanda looks around before screaming for her husband. "Jason! Come here!"

Jason comes over when he hears his wife beckoning him. He's not alone, though. I look up to see that Ben also sauntered over. Jason moves to sit next to his wife, which leaves the only open seat next to me. Ben comes over, and I try to make room for him on the small loveseat. It's a two-seater, and when he sits down, his thigh brushes against mine. I subtly try to move my leg, but he man-spreads, pressing his thigh against mine. The contact makes me feel hot and jittery. I feel my core ache, and I'm already getting wet. It's like he has my body trained to respond to his every touch, even if it's innocent. Except I know he's doing it deliberately.

I try to sneak a glance at his crotch, and I think I make out the subtle shape of his cock in his jeans. It makes me bite my lip as I imagine him being hard while sitting in front of our friends, who are now arguing about baby names. I feel a hand brush mine, and he slowly moves to wrap his pinky finger around mine in a sly handhold, and I feel my heart melting at the gesture.

I suddenly can't wait for everyone to leave so we can be alone again. The longer I sit next to Ben, the more turned on I get until I'm clenching my thighs to relieve some of the pressure. When I squirm a little, Ben looks over at me and smirks knowingly. I flush and curse him silently.

The bastard knows exactly what he's doing. Well, two can play that game. I move to reach across his body for my drink at the end of the table in front of him. In doing so, I place my hands on his thigh, my fingertips brushing the tip of his cock as I lean over to grab my drink. I hear him take in a sharp breath. When I move to sit back down, my finger strokes his tip for a couple of seconds before withdrawing. I swear I feel him vibrating with tension.

I smile smugly and take a sip of my drink, but almost spit it out when he leans over to whisper gruffly in my ear, "You're going to pay for that."

I try to stifle the shiver that passes through me. I take a few more sips from my glass of wine to cool down. It's suddenly so hot in here. I think I need to open the window and let some fresh air in. Yeah, that's exactly what I need to do.

I get up to crack open the window in the sunroom to let in the fresh air. The sunroom is empty, and it's quieter out here. I stay there for a moment, just trying to catch my breath. The hairs on my neck prickle, a silent alarm announcing Ben's presence. I didn't think he'd follow me out here, but now that he has, I'm breathless with anticipation.

He brushes a finger up my arm in a soft caress, the touch raising my temperature even more and sending my pulse to beat erratically. When he gets to my shoulder, his hand cups my upper arm to turn me around. He inches me backward until my back is up against the wall. He stares down at me intently, his expression unreadable in the dimly lit room.

Slowly, as if scared I'd bolt if he moved too quickly, he brings his head down until his lips hover right over mine. My hands reach up to place them on his chest, feeling the hard muscles of his pectorals. I swear I can also feel his frantic heartbeat beneath my palms. His lips are just mere millimeters away, and my lips part slightly. Our breaths mingle as we savor the electric moment, knowing that any of our friends could walk in on us at any point and discover our secret.

Finally, I tilt my chin up so that our lips meet, and I swear I see fireworks flash behind my closed eyelids. The sensation of falling while standing is dizzying as our lips take each other in hungrily, like we've been holding our breath underwater this whole time and are finally coming up for air. His tongue parts my lips and delves in possessively as if he's been waiting for this moment all night long, just like I have. I feel a sense of relief to be in his arms again. I move my arms up to wrap around his neck, and he's pushed up against my body as close as he can get against the wall.

I'm not sure how long we remain connected. We fervently kiss, aware discovery is imminent. In my wildest dreams, I never thought I would be in this predicament, standing here with my back against the wall and stealing kisses in the dark.

We finally break apart when the sounds of footsteps approaching grow near. He takes a few steps away from me to put some distance between us, and I see Jason's head appear behind Ben's shoulder.

"Hey, buddy! There you are! We're just about to head out. Amanda's pretty tired, so I need to get her to bed."

Ben stares at me for another moment, his tongue gently licking his lower lip before he turns around and does the guy hug thing that guys do to say goodbye. They exchange some words, and then Jason bids me farewell. I catch Amanda on her way out and give her a hug.

"You didn't get to try the cake!" I tell her, but she giggles and tells me she snuck a piece when I disappeared. She gives me a wink, and then they're out the door.

I hurry into the kitchen, where I had brought out the cake earlier. I place some candles on it and light it up. Silence falls, and someone dims the lights. Someone sings "Happy Birthday," and we're all chiming in, except Ben is nowhere to be found.

Where the heck did he go? After a minute of looking around for him, Ben comes out of his bedroom to a chorus of cheers. Everyone resumes their singing, and I present the cake decorated with birthday candles to him. Someone snaps a photo on their phone, and a flash goes off, but we only have eyes for each other.

We smile at each other like two lovesick fools, and then he mutters a soft thanks under his breath. I gesture to the cake with a head tilt to encourage him to blow out the candles. He takes in a breath, and I yell at him to stop.

"Wait! You need to make a wish before you blow out the candles!"

"Seriously?" Ben rolls his eyes at me.

"Seriously."

Ben pauses in contemplation, and then he takes a big breath, blowing out all the candles in one try. I hear the crowd clapping gleefully as I place the cake down on the table, handing the cake knife over to Ben to cut up and plate the cake while I hand them out.

When people taste the cake, their moans of appreciation make me giddy. I'm eager to try some, but unfortunately, there's only one piece remaining. The cake was a real hit, I guess. I look up at Ben, who's holding the last slice in his giant palm.

"Wanna share my piece, roomie?" His eyes twinkle in delight.

"Oh, no, that's o—" He shoves a piece of cake in my mouth, and I clamp my lips tight around the tines of the fork.

"Oh my god, it's so good." I moan as the chocolate flavors burst on my tongue.

"Keep making those noises, and everyone is going to know we're not just roomies," Ben growls softly as he feeds me another bite of cake. I try to not moan as he continues to alternate between taking small bites of the cake and feeding me.

Shortly after serving the cake, people began to leave. Many come up to give hugs and say goodbye before leaving. Before I know it, Ben and I are alone in our apartment. It's a mess, but I am too tired to clean.

Despite the mess, I feel the happiest I have been in such a long time.

26
Emily

Ben's birthday arrives a few days after our successful birthday/housewarming party. Well, at least I considered it successful, and it seemed like everyone had a good time. By the time everyone had left, we were both too exhausted to fool around. We both collapsed onto my bed in a pile of tangled limbs. I fell asleep with Ben's arms wrapped tightly around me and didn't wake until the sun was high in the sky the following day.

Though I had little to drink, I still felt the aftereffects of a long night of hosting. Running around to make sure everything was perfect was exhausting. Or I'm just getting old.

I groan and stretch my aching body. I accidentally knock Ben in the face with my outstretched arm and turn to apologize to him. He has one eye cracked open in a sleepy glare before his big arm reaches out to yank me so I'm lying half under him. We fell asleep briefly before he got up and made us a late lunch. It took most of the evening to clean up the apartment from all the empty drinks and trash that people left behind. Before long, we were back in bed.

The next few days pass in a blur of long workdays and busy routines. I've been trying to figure out what I might get Ben for his birthday today. I know he told me he didn't want any presents, but I think everyone deserves a present on their birthday to celebrate another year alive. It's impossible to decide, given the short time we've actually gotten to know each other. Plus, I don't want to come off like a crazy, clingy girlfriend. I know we said we'd keep things casual, and things have been working out for us so far.

That's how I find myself at the busy mall, running into shop after shop to figure out what someone would get their roommate who they kind of like and are also having lots of orgasms with. There isn't a handbook for this sort of thing, and I wish there were. It certainly would make my life a lot easier.

After a few hours of indecision riddled with crippling anxiety, I settle for a luxury shaving kit from one of the boutique barber shops. It smells good, and the kit seems really fancy, with a matching price tag. I know it can't be easy to maintain his neatly trimmed beard. The bonus is that it doesn't scream, "I'm crazy and might catch feelings for you."

The clerk hands me the hand-wrapped package in a paper bag and smiles in thanks. I grip the bag and stroll out of the mall. The location of the mall is not a very long drive from our apartment. Our location has so many perks that I find my new living situation even more exciting by the day. There are so many local activities, boutique stores, nightlife, and five-star restaurants; you name it, Bramblewood has it. Not to mention that my apartment is within minutes of the local highway, so I can be anywhere in the state in less than an hour.

I'm just pulling into our shared driveway, and I notice that Ben's already home.

Shit! How am I supposed to sneak this into the apartment without him seeing it? I improvise by shoving the bag into one of the other shopping bags so he can't see his gift.

I walk into the apartment, but Ben isn't anywhere to be found. I suspect he must be in his bedroom. He must have gotten out of work a little early. Tiptoeing quietly, I head to my bedroom and shove the bags into the closet. I pull out the new matching loungewear I bought from Victoria's Secret before closing the door. I quickly change out of my outfit and even change my underwear. Just in case we get frisky. Who doesn't feel good in fresh panties and cute new clothes?

I admire my ass in the mirror. These new jogger-style pants do a wonderful job of making it look perky. I spin in a circle and head out to find Ben. His bedroom door is ajar, but my knock is unanswered. I gently push the door open and find him spread out half-naked on top of his bed. He's passed out and gently snoring. He's wearing those irresistible gray sweatpants that do nothing to hide his half-erect cock.

I roll my lips and hover at the doorway. He looks like a snack with his muscles on display. I slowly creep over to the side of his bed, half expecting him to open his eyes and glare at me. When several moments pass, and he still hasn't stirred, I place a knee next to his hips. I take in a deep inhale and bask in his unique scent that sends tingles to my core, which is already getting wet with anticipation.

I lean over his body and give him a soft peck on his forehead, then his nose, and finally his lips. He stirs softly when I get to his lips and moans in his sleep. His eyes crack open, and he whispers my name like he's happy to see me. I give him another kiss on his lips, though it's firmer than the last. I pepper soft kisses along his jawline and down to his Adam's apple. I flick out my tongue in a teasing lick, and he groans at the contact.

"Emily, you're home." His voice is husky with sleep.

"Mmmhmm," I hum back in response.

His hands softly grasp me around my upper arms, but he doesn't stop me as I continue my exploration of his body. Kissing his pecs and teasing his nipples with my tongue, I give both equal attention. I straddle his hips while trying to keep most of my weight off him and feel his hard erection against my butt. I move down and lick in between each indent of his delicious abs and rub my lips softly over the trail of dark hair that leads down to his cock.

"What are you doing, Emily?" he rasps softly, voice still thick with sleep.

"Just saying happy birthday."

He hums in response, and I work his sweatpants down until his cock springs free. Apparently, he's going commando, which means less work for me. I reposition myself so I'm kneeling between his legs as I take in his hard cock. He continues to swell under my perusal like he can sense my stare. I tentatively reach out to grip the base of his cock and give it an experimental tug. Ben's answering moans are encouraging, and I continue with my ministrations. I lick my lips at the sight of pre-cum beading on the tip.

Before I can talk myself out of it, I'm leaning over and licking his tip and swirling my tongue around the head of his cock. Ben lets out a growled swear, and I feel his hands grip my hair in its ponytail. I take the tip of his cock into my mouth and suck.

"Fuck! Emily!" His hips buck up in response, and I move my mouth up and down the length of his cock. I use my hands to stroke him in a coordinated effort to bring him to climax. His hold on my hair tightens around the base of my ponytail, and I feel him guiding me at a fast pace. It gets sloppy quickly, with my saliva dripping down my chin and down the length of his cock. The lewd noises we're making are turning me on, and I know that I've made a mess in my clean underwear. I clench my thighs to ease the ache.

When I use my other hand to cup and tug on his balls, Ben loses any semblance of control. His hips pump up to meet my mouth, and he lets out a long groan.

"Fuck, I'm going to come!" he hisses in warning. I hold steady as he continues to pump in and out of my mouth, using me to get himself to the edge. As his cum sprays the back of my throat, I try to keep his load in my mouth until he finishes. I look up at him as his cock continues to twitch in my mouth. I wrap my lips around the head of his cock and give him one last suck before popping off. Maintaining his eye contact, I open my mouth to show him the mess he left.

He growls at me, and I close my mouth and swallow his load.

"Fuck, that's hot." He sits up and grabs my face in his hand, his thumb at the corner of my lips, and he wipes away the cum that dribbles out. He brings my face to his and kisses me, not caring that he can probably taste himself.

I've soaked through my panties at this point and am trembling with arousal. My hands grip his shoulders, and I climb onto his lap.

"Does someone need me to take care of this needy pussy?" he asks me when he finally breaks our kiss.

I nod desperately, and he flips us over before yanking off my pants. He leaves my panties on, and I swear I can feel more wetness trickle out at his intense stare.

"My, my, my, look at the mess you made."

I whimper when he leans down and kisses the mound of my pussy. It's so close to where I need him to touch that it feels agonizing. I'm bucking my hips to move him closer to my clit, but he pins my hips down with an arm braced across my stomach.

"Stay still, or you won't get to come."

If I were coherent, I would probably rear up and swear at him, but I'm so turned on that I just want to get off.

He gives my panty-clad pussy a long lick until he reaches my clit where he gives it a soft kiss, followed by a few flicks of his tongue. With his arm braced on my belly, I can't really move, which drives me even crazier with need.

"Please," I whimper.

"Hmm... I love it when you beg."

He finally pulls my panties aside and feasts on my pussy. When I say feast, I mean the man goes to town licking me and getting my juices all over his face. He inserts a finger in me and starts thrusting it in and out while his tongue flicks at my clit at a relentless rhythm. I know I'm keening and making all kinds of unabashed noises, and as he inserts a second finger, I feel my thighs shake. He hooks his fingers and continues his assault on my clit, and I feel an odd pressure in my belly.

"Oh god, I think I'm going to come," I warn him breathlessly.

"Come for me," he demands and adds a third finger into the mix. With the constant ministrations on my clit combined with his hooked fingers on my G-spot, I feel myself explode, but it feels different from any other time. The pressure is gone, and the orgasm rolls through me just as I feel fluid squirting out.

"Ah, fuck yeah, you made such a mess. Good girl. Give it all to me."

My thighs shake as my orgasm drags on. The edges of my vision blacken, and I'm not even sure I'm still breathing. When I catch my breath, I realize the bed is much wetter than it should be.

Oh god, did I pee on the bed? I sit up in a panic and look at the giant wet spot between my legs. Ben wipes his face with the back of his arm and grins at me.

"First time squirting, I take it."

I groan and plop back on the bed, covering my face with my hands. He gives my pussy a slap and fixes my panties as I yelp.

As he lies down next to me, I finally remember why I had come in to find him.

"Happy birthday, roomie." I smile dreamily at him.

"Oh, it's a happy birthday, alright," he says, both of us grinning like a pair of lovesick fools.

27
Emily

"What do you think about this?" I ask Ben, holding up a blown glass ornament in the shape of a penis. He looks at the item in my hand and shakes his head, chuckling softly under his breath.

We're at the local farmer's market I heard about when I was getting a cup of coffee at the cute coffee shop down the street known for its specialty lattes. Today's flavor of the day is peppermint mocha. I'm taking small sips and browsing all the local shops. Ben looks mildly bored, but he hasn't complained, so I hope it's not torturous to him.

Earlier this morning over breakfast, I mentioned to him that I wanted to check the market and see what all the fuss was about. While I was at the sink washing the dishes, I felt his arms come around my shoulders, and he kissed the top of my head. He squeezed me and told me to let him know when I was leaving.

I thought he had just wanted to know when I was out of the apartment, so when I announced I was leaving, I was shocked to find him dressed.

"I'll drive." He took my hand and drove us downtown, following the directions on my phone's navigation system, and here we are. Enjoying a lazy Sunday doing what I imagine couples who have been together for a while do. I've passed by many hand-holding couples and some dragging a disgruntled husband, and it makes me wonder if Ben and I could ever get to this place where we'd be one of those hand-holding couples. Or, worse, the disgruntled duo.

I froze, lost in thought. If I really try, I can imagine the two of us together. The timing seems wrong, though. Maybe we could be happy together if we don't bungle things up.

Or maybe, just maybe, the universe brought us together for this exact moment. But am I ready to let someone into my heart again after what I just went through? Could I trust anyone else ever again? I couldn't imagine things ending badly with Ben and being forced to move. Again. It would be like I'm back at square one.

Can I handle that? Is it worth the possible heartbreak?

My thoughts swirl in my head like a chaotic storm, a tempest of anxieties and uncertainties, leaving me disoriented and reeling. The turbulence overwhelms my senses, each thought is a sharp gust of wind, tossing me about like a leaf in a storm. I'm finding it hard to keep my cool amidst all the chaos.

I'm startled out of my thoughts when I feel Ben lift my chin with a light touch. I meet his worried gaze and give him a small smile.

"Hey, tiger. Lost in thought again? You okay, babe?"

My eyes widen slightly. Did he just call me babe?

"Um… yeah, I'm fine," I lie through my teeth.

He looks at me suspiciously but doesn't call me out before he grabs my hand to urge me along. I hadn't realized I had stopped walking and was standing in the middle of the walkway. We leave after another hour. I purchased some earrings from a local jeweler and a new romance book that one of the book clubs on wheels was selling.

His hand, rough against mine, was a grounding, comforting presence. Like an anchor, it keeps me from floating away, a steady presence in my turbulent thoughts.

❦ ❦ ❦ ❦ ❦

That night, after another home-cooked meal of shrimp and grits, courtesy of Ben's surprising culinary skills, we both settle in to watch another movie on Netflix. I'm lying down on one end of the couch with my sock-clad feet resting on Ben's lap. He has one hand resting on my leg, and the other is using the remote to flick through our options. After what feels like hours later, we select an action movie featuring Jason Bourne. As the movie starts, I wiggle on the couch to get comfortable, my foot accidentally brushing his half-erect cock. Geez, is he always hard?

He slaps his hand on my foot to stop me from further wiggling it and shoots me an amused stare.

"Careful, tiger, or we won't be watching the movie after all."

"Well, maybe I don't want to watch the movie." My reply is sassy and taunting. I yelp when he yanks on my calf and drags me down to the couch so I'm closer to him. He spreads my legs, leans over me, and settles his hips between my thighs. My breath hitches, accelerating with the sudden closeness of his warm body; the woodsy scent of his cologne, sharp and intoxicating, makes my head swim.

"And what is it you want to do instead, hmmm?" He leans in and softly kisses my collarbone, making me whimper in response. He slowly glides his lips across my pebbled skin. I bare my neck in a silent plea for him to continue. His tongue flicks out to lick the junction where my shoulder meets, and I gasp. He hums his pleasure and continues his journey until he's mere inches from my lips.

His forehead rests on mine, a silent moment of connection. Our breaths mingle in the space between us, ragged and quick, creating a symphony of intimacy. Exhilaration surges inside of me like a bright, fierce flame igniting within. Burning away all of my doubts in the face of the unknown. Come what may, I know with absolute certainty, a feeling as solid as the earth beneath us, that we were in this together.

I'm not sure whether it is one of us or both, but our lips meet like colliding storm clouds. My heart pounds loudly in my ears. I don't know where he ends and I begin. I never want this moment to end.

Our tongues duel in a seductive dance for dominance, and I concede as he uses a rough hand to tip my head back to devour me. I groan, and my roaming hands find themselves around his neck, buried tightly in his soft curls. His kiss feels endless, and I'm lost in the abyss of pleasure. Warmth pools at my center, and the resulting wetness would be embarrassing if I didn't know how much it drives Ben wild.

He breaks off the kiss and bares my stomach, placing a soft kiss right below my navel. He shoves my shirt up over my chest to expose my heaving breasts, nipples peaking from arousal. His groan is the only answer I need to know if my small chest is a turn-on for him. He pulls the cups of my bra down to expose one nipple before lurching up to capture the brown peak in his hot mouth.

"Oh, fuck!" I never realized my nipples were so sensitive as he sucks and laves at me. After he's satisfied that he's given it enough attention, he pulls the cup from my other breast down and gives it the same attention. I know that I'm soaked, and my skin feels too tight. I need release, and I need to be filled. There's an emptiness in my core that only he can fill.

"Please, Ben." My whispered pleas cause him to lift his head, and the look of pure hunger on his face breaks my resolve.

"Please what, tiger? What do you need?" His voice is husky from pleasure.

"Please, I need you." His hum of satisfaction sets me at ease. I know he wants this as much as I do, judging by the hard erection that's tenting his pants. He helps me out of my shirt and bra and sits back on his heels. Slowly, he glides his fingertips to the waist-band of my pants and inches them off my hips. I bend my knees as he slips them off before tossing them to the side. I'm left bare in my powder blue boy shorts. His hungry gaze devours my almost nude body, and I would feel exposed if not for the voracity of his need.

After what feels like an eternity of us taking each other in, Ben reaches behind his neck and yanks his shirt off over his head. He pulls his sweatpants down before pausing and cursing softly.

"What's the matter?" I sit up on my elbows to see him better. He has his head back, and the muscles in his neck are strained. He blows out a breath and looks at me apologetically. My heart plummets to my stomach.

"I don't have any condoms." His tone is remorseful.

I bite my lower lip as I consider our options. "I'm clean, and I'm on birth control... I mean, if you're comfortable..."

His gaze intensifies as he studies me.

"I got tested a few weeks ago before we moved in and haven't been with anyone since. I'm clean if you're sure about this."

I nod my head, and suddenly, he pulls me toward him, grip-ping my outer thighs so I'm flat on my back again. My under-wear is gone before I know it. He rears up over me with arms braced on either side of my head. Our chests are millimeters from touching. The air crackles with unspoken tension, a palpable energy humming between us, the silence punctuated by the rapid beat of my heart.

He lowers his upper body down slowly as if he is afraid that any sudden movement would send me running away from him. He rests a forearm by my head and uses the other to guide the head of his cock at my slick entrance. The heat of his cock begging for entry sends another rush of arousal to my center. He rubs his cock up and down my slit.

"You're so wet for me. My cock is soaked in your juices, and

I'm not even inside you yet," he growled. "You sure? Last chance."

I wrap my arms around his back and bring my legs to wrap around his hips, giving him no room to escape.

"Yes, I'm sure. I want you inside me. Now," I demand. I'm lost in the sexual haze that's enveloped us both.

He guides the tip of his cock back to my entrance, and my hips lift automatically as he enters me in one swift movement. I gasp at the sudden intrusion, and Ben groans. He drops his forehead to mine, our quickened breaths mingling between us. He leans down and kisses my lips sweetly as he lets my body adjust to his intrusion. I feel so full, and I never realized how empty I felt until this moment.

"Ready, tiger?" he asks gruffly before slowly retreating. I moan as he pumps back into me, and my legs climb higher around his waist to make more room for him. His pace quickens, and I match his thrusts with equal vehemence. Our moans of pleasure mix in with the movie, and I'm glad for the background noise, as I'm sure the downstairs neighbor can hear us.

"Fuck, you feel so good around my cock." Ben hits a sensitive spot when he thrusts hard, and my hips arch as I gasp in response.

"Oh god. I think I'm going to come."

"Come on my cock, baby."

He maintains a relentless pace, his cock and pelvis hitting at just the right angle. The pressure intensifies to a blistering height, and I scream in ecstasy as my core clenches around his cock in an earth-shattering orgasm. My legs shake from the intensity, and Ben continues his pace until the last of the aftershocks are gone.

"Fuck, that was hot," he groans and changes his angle so he's somehow buried even deeper than I thought possible. "Give me one more, baby."

My nails rake down his back, my head shaking side to side as I feel the telltale signs of another rapidly approaching orgasm.

His fingers find my clit. The touch sends me hurdling over the precipice. My body seizes with another orgasm. Ben's hips stutter jerkily as I milk his cock. He lets out a heavy groan as he comes. The sensation of him coming inside of me makes my muscles contract around him. Almost like my body was trying to squeeze every last drop out of his hard cock.

When my soul returns to my body, I realize Ben has me cradled in his chest with one arm around my shoulders and his head resting next to my ear. We're both still breathing heavily, and I relax my tight hold on his back.

"Wow."

He lifts his head, looks at me for bated breath, and then chuckles softly. "Yeah. Wow."

He separates our bodies gingerly, and I whimper as his body slips out of mine, already missing his fullness. I startle in awareness as I feel his cum leaking out of me. My eyes are wide with panic, but before I can move, Ben grabs his discarded shirt and cleans me up with rapt attention.

"Mmm... I love seeing my cum dripping out of this needy pussy. I might have to fill it up again just to see this every time." I flush with both heat and embarrassment. Why does that turn me on so much? The thought of having someone come inside me before was always disgusting to me. Logan always pulled out and came on my belly or back, but he never dared to come inside of me. I'm surprised by how wet and sticky everything feels, but knowing that it turns Ben on makes me eager for it to happen again. This is probably some kind of kink that I haven't read about yet, but I'll need to find some new reading material, STAT!

Once I'm cleaned up to Ben's satisfaction, he moves to get up but tells me not to move a muscle. He covers me with a blanket draped over the side of the couch and disappears to the bathroom. I hear the water running before he returns with a wet towel in one hand. He moves the blanket so I'm bared to him again before using the warmed towel to clean between my legs with tenderness. I gasp and arch away when his hands brush my overly sensitive clit. He covers my body with the blanket again and grabs the dirty shirt.

"Stay here," he instructs as he disappears around the corner. I'm lying naked on the couch with a blanket to keep me warm in the most amazing post-coital fog of my life. Ben comes back, scoops me up in his arms, and heads to my bedroom. He's pulled the covers back and lays me down gently before climbing in.

I fall asleep to the sound of his heartbeats, and I feel like the luckiest person in the world.

28

Emily

I might have unlocked a caged beast. Ever since we had sex on the couch a few nights ago, Ben has been insatiable. We ended up both calling out of work the following day and spent the time alternating between fucking each other's brains out or eating to replenish our energy stores, only to go back at it like rabbits in the springtime.

I've lost track of the number of times he's made me come, but I know that it's many more times than he has. It's like he's a man possessed and obsessed with making me come. We have fucked in every single room in the apartment, in every imaginable position, and some new ones I had never tried before. By the time it was evening, I had to tap out and beg for rest. My poor vagina was so overworked she did not know what was happening.

We're getting ready to visit Jason and Amanda at the hospital. Their son was born last night, and we each got a text from the parents with adorable newborn photos attached. I'm pulling an oversized sweater over my head when I hear Ben open my bedroom door. I can feel the heat of his gaze on me, and sure enough, when my vision clears, he's laser-focused on me. I put my hands up in a gesture to help ward him off.

"If we don't leave right now, we'll never leave the apartment."

I back away as he slowly advances, and my back hits my dresser.

"Ben! I'm serious! We need to go now." He approaches me and cages me in with his warm body. He bends his head down so his nose is grazing my ear as he takes a deep breath. After a moment, he exhales in a huff and leaves a chaste kiss on my forehead.

"Fine. You're right. Get your sweet ass in my car before I change my mind."

I fled from him, the sound of his amused laughter ringing in my ears. His joy resonates within me, a warm hum vibrating deep in my chest, like a sunbeam bursting through the clouds and filling my body with his warmth and light.

ɲ ɲ ɳ ŋ ̃

"He is so cute!" I gush over the less-than-twenty-four-hour-old baby swaddled and cradled in my arms. Amanda gave birth to sweet baby Alexander Joseph, and she barely looks like she broke a sweat. I swear, she always looks good, even on her worst days. Something I can't ever claim, but at least today, I got dressed and left the apartment.

I'm sitting in the uncomfortable armchair while the two men chatter in the corner. Looking down at the little bundle of joy in my arms, I get a sensation I've never felt before. I wonder what it would be like to hold *my* bundle of joy in my arms. I never wanted to have children before. I've always known that I enjoy my independent life, free from the worries of childcare. My traumatic childhood and lack of parental contact likely explain my aversion to having children.

But sitting here, in this moment, with another woman's child in my arms, I feel a tug at my psyche. Maybe the reason I could never see myself having children before also had to do with the guys I was dating. I could never picture co-parenting with anyone else.

With Ben, though, I can see a fuzzy future of the two of us with a couple of kids. The thought shocks me so much that I feel my body stiffen.

Slowly, I raise my head, and our eyes meet. A jolt of awareness, like a sudden electric current, passes between us. His expression softens as he studies me intently. His gaze roams over me as I cradle the sleeping baby with his tiny hand gripping my finger tightly. Ben's eyes sparkle with intense passion at the sight, and I shiver in response.

I swear he has the same thought process before Jason's loud voice breaks our staring match.

"How's the apartment treating you guys?" Jason looks at me, and I'm sure he doesn't miss the way Ben was staring at me.

"It's great," Ben answers with a sly grin.

I duck my head to hide my blush and pretend to coo over the snoring baby. We keep the visit short as other visitors trickle in. I hand the baby back to Amanda and give her a one-arm hug. Before I let her go, she turns to look at me and says softly under her breath, "Looks like you two are getting along."

I pull away, and she smirks at me. I didn't think Ben and I were obvious, but I guess we weren't as discreet as we thought we were.

"We're just friends," I deny and then rush out of the room. I don't miss Amanda's wink at my denial. I was always a terrible liar.

29
Emily

The weeks fly by as winter gives way to spring. I know the warming weather is only a small part of why I'm feeling hopeful and refreshed lately. It might have something to do with my career change, which has been less soul-sucking and more of what I imagined myself doing when I went to school to be a nurse. I feel like the work I do has measurable outcomes in terms of people getting better and being able to move on with their lives. Don't get me wrong; there are many sad cases of patients not surviving the trauma their bodies endured, and some lives are lost, but the happy endings keep me going.

It probably also has to do with my handsome roommate, who has been spending more time in my bed than his own. His bedroom acts more like a closet than a sleeping space at this point. You won't hear me complaining about it. I'm getting spoiled with his attention, and the early morning orgasms help set the mood for the rest of the day.

We have been lost in our own world, stuck inside an insulated bubble of our own making, and while we planned to explore our new town, we spent most of our time together in our cozy apartment. We alternate between watching movies or the latest documentary series, playing Mario Kart, or quietly spending time on the couch together. I like to read with my feet resting in his lap while he settles in with his laptop to get some work done. Regardless of what we're doing, we're almost always touching each other. It's like we both can't get enough of the other. And, mostly, we can now go at least several hours before we're both naked.

However, he's banned from the sunroom during my yoga practice because the sight of me in downward dog is too tempting for him to resist. The constant feeling of eyes on your ass makes achieving a state of zen nearly impossible. Of course, I don't help matters by taunting him with provocative poses— slow, deliberate movements meant to ignite the smoldering embers of his already simmering arousal. The way his jaw clenches, his eyes darkening with barely suppressed desire, sends an illicit thrill through me. I know I'm playing with fire.

Tonight, we have plans to go to a surprise birthday party my best friend from college, Nikki, is throwing for her fiancé, Chris. Chris is turning thirty at the end of the month, and they're getting married next winter. I still haven't told her about Ben, and the last time I saw the pair was at our party a couple of months ago. It's not that I'm ashamed of how things progressed. If anything, I've been protective of our time together. I've enjoyed getting to know Ben better without the world weighing in on our unconventional union. I know people will have opinions. I just don't want to hear them.

We're both happy and don't expect more from each other. It's a mutual understanding, given how we ended up under the same roof. I'm sure we will have to discuss it eventually, but there's no rush.

Ben drives us to the clubhouse that Nikki rented for the party. Since it's a surprise party, she had asked everyone to park on the backside of the building. We brought desserts, which Ben grabs from his trunk before putting an arm around my shoulders. He only lets go of me to open the door for me. The space is large and already mostly decorated. Nikki sees me coming in and runs over to give me a big hug.

"Hey, you guys! I'm so happy you're here!" She ushers us in and instructs us on where to put the desserts. She also puts us to work on finishing the decorations. Before we know it, she's telling everyone to be quiet as Chris is about to walk in. When the door opens, everyone shouts an exuberant "surprise" to a shocked Chris before Nikki wanders over, and they embrace. It's a touching moment between them, and they break apart to greet the rest of the guests.

While the partygoers are mostly Nikki and Chris' friends, whom I'm familiar with, Ben is less acquainted with the people at the party. Even though he doesn't know most of the people here, he seems at ease making conversations and meeting new people. I didn't even realize I was worrying about him being around people he didn't know and thought he'd be stuck to my side the whole time. It reminds me of how Logan acted in these types of scenarios and how he always pouted about not knowing anyone.

We spend the time talking to Nikki and Chris and playing drinking games. Ben and I partner up to play beer pong, and though we lose horribly, it is the most fun I've had playing this game in a while. He hugs me and gives me a quick kiss on the lips before breaking apart. I get lost in the moment and don't even think about it until Nikki gasps and yells across the room, "I knew it!"

I turn guiltily to her and give her a sheepish smile and shrug. She grabs my arm and gives Ben a stern look before pulling me to a corner of the room.

"Spill!" she demands.

I hold up my hands in a placating gesture but end up telling her everything. When I'm done, I let out a breath of relief. It feels good to finally tell someone. I know Nikki isn't the type of person to judge, but it wasn't how I had wanted people to find out about us.

"Is he good to you?" she asks, the concern evident on her face. Nikki has been my best friend since freshman year of college. She's seen me go through so many ups and downs in that time. I know she's only worried about me and wants what's best for me.

"Yes. He's so good to me," I respond without hesitation.

"I always knew you guys would end up together." The confusion must be apparent on my face as she continues, "You and Logan never made sense together. Your personalities clashed. You're hot, and he's cold. He was also a jerk." She gives me a knowing look, and I nod in agreement. I'm done making excuses for Logan. He had been a shitty boyfriend and an awful friend to me.

"But Ben is like your perfect match. It's like you're two peas in a pod. Cut from the same cloth. And I can see he makes you happy." Nikki tears up as she holds my hands. I sniff at the unexpected warmth that spreads through my chest at her insight.

She hugs me and tells me she can't wait for our wedding invite before bouncing away to talk to the other guests. I'm left with my thoughts reeling. How long did people know that Logan and I wouldn't make it? Why didn't anyone tell me sooner? Could I have saved myself some heartbreak and embarrassment? Or did it all happen as it should?

I know what she means about Logan. He was stiff and awkward in most situations. He always felt uncomfortable in a crowd of people he didn't know. I always wondered if it had anything to do with being a cop and seeing the seedier side of humanity. Logan had always preferred spending time with his friends.

I never noticed how it impacted me until I saw how Ben blends in effortlessly with virtual strangers. He's friendly to everyone he meets. Ben strikes up conversation with anyone and has a way of making you feel like the center of his attention. I watch him in awe as he talks to Sasha, who is hanging on to his every word.

I'm lost in thought for the rest of the night and am quiet on the short ride back to our apartment. Ben holds my hand as he drives but otherwise leaves me alone to my own thoughts. When we get inside our apartment, he turns to me, gives me a big bear hug, and kisses the top of my head.

"Penny for your thoughts?" He pulls away and looks at me worriedly.

"Nikki knows about us," I say simply, and he smiles softly.

"Yeah, I know. She talked to me, too."

I raise my eyebrows. I don't remember seeing them talking.

"You were in the bathroom," he clarifies before continuing, "She wanted to let me know that if I hurt you, she'd cut off my balls and make me eat them." He winces and cups a hand around his genitals. "I believe her."

I laugh and reach up on my tiptoes to kiss him. When our lips part, we share a smile before I ask tentatively, "Are you okay with people knowing about us being together?"

"Of course." He didn't even have to think about it. "I've wanted to tell everyone that you're mine for months, but I knew you needed time."

I pull back from Ben to look at him closely.

"Months?"

He nods slowly. "Yeah. At the risk of sounding cheesy… Do you want to go steady with me? Be my girlfriend?"

I stare at him wide-eyed for a moment before smiling. "Go steady, huh?"

He chuckles and grips the back of my neck with his giant hand. "So, what's the answer, babe?"

"I think we've been going steady for months now." I bring my arms up and wrap them around his neck. He bends down and picks me up, and I wrap my legs around his waist as he carries me to my bedroom.

"Let's seal the deal, shall we?"

Ben tosses me onto the bed, and I bounce a little. He gets to work, getting me out of my clothes while I help unbutton his jeans. He pushes my hands out of the way and yanks his pants down, along with his boxers. His muscled arm sweeps behind his head, pulling his sweater off in one motion.

We both take in the other person. I'm still in my bra and panties, but I know that won't last much longer. Then, as if the spell is broken, he leaps at me with a soft growl, and I fall back with a laugh. The laugh quickly turns into a moan when he places soft kisses along my neck and collarbone while ridding me of my bra. He pulls my body up higher in the bed so our feet aren't dangling off the edge, and he works his way down my body, pulling off my panties. I bend my knees to help him, and he tosses the offending material across the room.

"Mine," he says in a deep, husky voice laced with desire. He kisses me deeply, our tongues dancing and dueling for dominance. He breaks the kiss and flips me over onto my belly, and I yelp. "I love this sweet ass," he says gruffly as he grabs two handfuls and squeezes my cheeks with rough hands, which sends a shock of arousal to my pussy. He pushes me so my head is down and my ass is up in the air as he trails kisses to my core. I feel the telltale signs of wetness dripping from my cunt.

"Look how wet you are for me." He flicks a tongue out and groans as he tastes my arousal. "I love the way you taste."

With his nose nudging my asshole, he burrows his face into my pussy as he licks, kisses, and tortures me until I reach a screaming orgasm with shocking speed.

"Must be a record," he says smugly as he kneels behind me and lines himself up at my entrance. I feel him notch the head of his cock as he enters me while the aftershocks of my orgasm still pulse through me. I gasp at his intrusion, and we both groan when he's fully seated inside me. In this position, he feels huge as his cock stretches me. I'm straddling the line of pain and pleasure with his cock buried so deep inside of me. He pulls out slightly, then pulls me up, pressing my back against his chest. He keeps one arm banded around my chest with a hand gripping my throat and the other hand rubbing my clit as he thrusts up into me.

"You're mine," he growls into my ear. I can barely move to meet his thrusts, and he has complete control over my body in this position. I reach behind me with one hand and bury it in his hair as I throw my head back on his shoulders and enjoy the sensation of him rubbing against my G-spot. Before Ben, I never knew I even had a G-spot, and now I'm getting familiar with the leg-shaking sensation of him hitting it. It's almost guaranteed to make me squirt with the intense orgasm that's sure to come if he keeps up his pace combined with him rubbing my clit and the added stimulation of his hard grip around my neck. It's tight enough to restrict my breathing but not enough that I can't breathe.

Ben keeps up the relentless torture until I fall apart again for him. When he's satisfied that he's prolonged my orgasm as much as possible, he groans and pushes me down, pounding into me as I brace myself on my forearms. He comes with a loud groan, and I feel his seed pulsing inside of me. We both collapse into boneless, panting heaps on my bed.

"I think we need to invest in new bed sheets," I finally say, and we both laugh.

After cleaning up and changing the sheets, we finally snuggle up in bed.

My head rests on his hard chest, and I can hear the steady thump-thump of his heart against my ear. His steady heartbeat is a calming rhythm. I wrestle with my thoughts, a knot of anxiety tightening in my chest before blurting out, "Can I tell you a secret?"

"Hmm?" Though his voice was heavy with sleep, I felt his hand gently push my hair from my face.

"I've had a crush on you for a while. Like years," I hastily confess before I lose my nerve. "Ever since we met on Memorial Day five years ago at Jason's pool party."

Ben remained silent, and when I looked up, I saw him staring at me thoughtfully.

"I remember the party." Ben's words hit me like a ton of bricks, each syllable sharp and cutting. "I was with Melissa... We had just started dating."

I'm questioning again if there's a reason behind everything. What if he wasn't in a relationship then? Would we be together? I underestimated the chemistry between us at our first meeting; however, his relationship with another woman made me keep my distance. Then, several years later, I met Logan. And the rest was history.

I shift in bed, and Ben snuggles close behind. His warm chest against my back gave me a feeling of safety and comfort.

When I hear Ben's soft snores, I turn around to look at his sleeping face. He looks so relaxed in his sleep. The dim lighting casts his face in shadows, and I softly trace my hands along his jawline.

"I think you've been mine for a while," I say to his sleeping form and plant a whisper of a kiss against his soft, plump lips. He pulls me close as I burrow into his arms.

"Mmmhmm. Love you," he mumbles sleepily, and my eyes widen in shock.

There's no way he loves me, right? He's probably dreaming about his ex-fiancée. Did my confession stir up memories of her? The thought sours my mood, and my heart sinks. I know it's too soon to be professing love for one another. It hasn't even been six months since their engagement ended, yet the thought of him still in love with his ex makes me want to scratch her eyes out. It makes me want to curl up and lick my own wounds. I want to rage and break things and yell at him. He can't love her because he loves me... Does he love me?

I wiggle out of his arms and turn my back to him. I know nothing good can come of this downward spiral I'm in. Knowing I have an early morning, I take some deep breaths and try to sleep. Eventually, I fall asleep to thoughts of what our future might look like.

30

Ben

I wake up alone. Not even the cats are sleeping with me. I had gotten used to falling asleep with my arms wrapped tightly around a snoring Emily while Buffy and Spike surrounded us. It's rare that I wake up after Emily, and I wonder if she's still in the apartment.

I strain my ears but don't hear anything.

My phone was discarded with my jeans the night before. I groan as I lean over the side of the bed and pull my phone out of the back pocket.

I see several notifications, including new messages. When I open them, I quickly realize that they aren't from Emily. I rub my eyes as if I could erase the image of the message from my mind.

I knew she had been too quiet, and it was only a matter of time before she would start messaging me again. I need to put an end to this and make sure Melissa knows without a doubt that we are never, ever getting back together.

I pull on my hair as the catchy song echoes in my sleepy mind. Maybe I should play the song on repeat so she catches my drift.

Reluctantly, I reply to Melissa's message and groan at the mess I created.

I check my other messages, and sure enough, there is one from Emily saying she went to hot yoga and she'd be back for lunchtime. She added some kissy face emojis at the end of her message, making me smile.

I shoot her a quick reply to let her know I saw her message. I'm thankful to be alone as a goofy smile spreads across my face. I know I'll see Emily again soon, but I miss her already.

I'm shocked by how much I miss her. We've only been together for a few months, but it feels like years. In the privacy of our apartment, we've found a sanctuary to delve into our emotions and deepen our connection. Though my feelings for her are intense, everything feels right. My life feels like it's all clicking into place for the very first time.

Her confession last night made me realize how little control we have over our lives. Had I not been in a relationship when I met Emily, we would likely have ended up together. I remember the day we met clearly. It was the first time I was disappointed at being in a relationship with Melissa. To make up for the guilt, I threw myself into our relationship. I know I'm responsible for our ruin; it was inevitable from the start.

It appears the universe is offering me a do-over, and I intend to make the most of it. It's a terrifying sensation, a gut-wrenching blend of fear and a fragile, flickering hope. I am determined not to fuck things up with Emily.

I hop in the shower and get ready, barely resisting the urge to rub one out to thoughts of Emily on her knees—again. I needed to get a move on so I could be back by the time Emily returned.

Pulling out of the driveway, I notice a familiar silver sedan parked at the end of the street. I drive past it slowly, making a note of the license plate, and head to the cafe.

❦ ❦ ❦ ❦ ❦

I walk into the small cafe and spot Melissa sitting against the wall in the back. I make my way over to her and suppress the grimace when she waves me over excitedly. It is probably misleading to agree to meet with her, but what I have to say needs to be done in person. I should have said it months ago.

"Ben! Hi! Thank you for meeting with me on such short notice." Melissa stands up as if to hug me, but I promptly sit down. I don't want there to be any misunderstandings about the meeting.

"Hey, Melissa." I offer a tight-lipped smile as she takes her seat across from me.

She fiddles with her coffee cup, suddenly unsure of herself.

"Listen, we need to talk." The words sound harsh even to my own ears, and I suppress a groan.

"What is it?" Melissa sits up straight, hope shining in her eyes.

"I should have done this months ago, but… Anyways, it's over, and I don't want to keep stringing you along."

I watch as the words sink in and resist the urge to reach over the table to comfort her. Melissa and I have so much history together, and the last thing I ever wanted to do was hurt her. But I know that not having a clean break has been doing so much damage.

"Oh." Melissa sinks back in her seat. "I see."

"You can keep the ring," I offer as an olive branch.

It was the wrong thing to say as anger morphs her features.

"Keep the ring? Of course, I'm keeping the ring!" Melissa stands up, and the next thing I know, she's pulling off the cap of her coffee and tossing its contents on my face.

I'm shocked into silence as the other patrons gasp at

Melissa's action. She slams the empty cup on the table and storms off.

A barista walks over with a handful of paper towels, a mop, and a grimace. I accept the paper towels gratefully and try to clean up the mess. Thankfully, it was iced coffee, so I didn't have to worry about getting burned by scalding liquid.

"That was rough," the barista comments as he starts to mop up the ground.

"Yeah. But I deserved it."

The barista nods at me as if he knew that was the case.

I reek of French vanilla when I finally get back to the apartment. Emily's car is in the driveway, so I know she's home. There was no way of hiding what happened since I didn't have a spare shirt to change into on the way home.

When I walk into the apartment, Emily has music playing as she vacuums. I can hear her moving around as I slowly make my way up the stairs.

She startles when she spots me covered in coffee stains.

"What happened to you?" She gasps as a hand covers her mouth in shock.

"Let me shower, and I'll tell you."

Emily nods, and I give her a peck on her nose before making my way into the bathroom.

By the time I'm showered and dressed, I find Emily waiting for me in the living room. She has an episode of Friends playing while Buffy sleeps on her lap. Spike is sleeping in a sunny spot across the back of the couch.

I run my hands through my damp hair anxiously. I'm not sure how this is going to go, but I know it's time to come clean. I move to sit across from her, and Emily notices the distance I purposely left between us. She sits up straighter, dislodging Buffy, who yowls in protest.

"What is it?" Her brows furrow in concern.

"I need to tell you something," I start, hands clenched in my lap. I take in a deep breath and tell her everything. "I haven't been completely honest with you."

I can see her anxiety mounting, and I gesture with my hands for her to wait.

"I just saw Melissa. She's the one who threw her coffee at me."

"Melissa? Your ex?" Emily pales, the color draining from her face as she takes in my words.

"It was nothing. I needed to see her in person to tell her that things were definitely over for us."

"What do you mean? I thought you guys have been over?"

"Yes and… no." I sigh and run my hands across my face. "You know that I broke off the engagement back in October."

Emily nods for me to continue.

"Well… it wasn't the last time that we…"

"You guys had sex?" She gapes at me, and I feel like the biggest dirtbag in the entire universe.

"Yes." I hang my head in shame.

"Oh my god." I glance up to see she's covered her mouth with her hands in horror.

"It was just the one time, and I knew it was a mistake," I rush to explain, but I don't know if my words are making things worse.

"One time?" Her throat bobs as she gulps.

"Yes, only once. In November. Before you and I even moved in together." My leg bounces in agitation. The urge to rush to her and hold her in my arms is impossible to ignore.

"Oh. Okay." She seems unsure what to do with the news.

"That's not all. Melissa has been messaging me since then. I've ignored all of her messages until today."

"Today. Why today?"

That was a good question, but I'm not sure she's ready for that answer. If anything, I might send her running scared if I admit how I really feel about her.

"I needed her to know that I was never getting back together with her." I gestured to myself, indicating my fresh change of clothes. "She obviously wasn't happy with the news."

"Oh." Her tense shoulders relax.

"Say something," I plead as I study her guarded expression.

After a contemplative moment, she looks at me, and I swear I feel her digging through the depths of my entire existence with her beautiful brown eyes.

"Do you still love her?"

"No." I shake my head. "It was a moment of weakness, but I don't love her. I haven't loved her in a very long time."

Emily nods absently and pets Buffy as she considers my words.

"Okay." She licks her dry lips.

"Okay?"

"I believe you." She offers a tentative smile.

Hearing those words does something to me. My heart, which had been weighed down with guilt, feels lighter with her acceptance. I had expected Emily to cry or, hell, yell at me for keeping this from her, but she'd done neither of those things.

I've been so conditioned to expect the worst from women, so I'm not sure how to handle Emily's acceptance. Did she forgive me for keeping the messages from her? I hope so.

"Oh, can I ask you something?"

"Yeah. Anything."

"Why do you call me tiger?"

"Well, for starters, it's because you're fierce like one." I pause as I think about my next words. "And I admire your strength in being able to pick yourself up and move on. I don't think a lot of people could have done what you did in your situation."

"You really think so?" She bites her lips as she considers my words.

"Yeah, I do." I stand up. I want to go to her, but I also respect that she may need some space from me right now. She stares up at me, and I fall into her eyes.

She stands up slowly, picking up Buffy and setting her to the side. She takes a step toward me, and I lurch forward and embrace her. I hug her to my chest, breathing in her scent. It feels like the first breath I've been able to take all day.

"I'm sorry for not telling you sooner," I murmur into her soft hair.

"I'm disappointed you didn't tell me sooner," she admits, her words muffled against my chest.

"I know."

I vow in that moment that I would never disappoint her ever again.

31
Emily

Spring is in full force, with birds chirping outside our windows. The weather has warmed up significantly, and the brighter sunshine days have been a welcomed relief. I wouldn't mind spring so much if it weren't for all the rainy days. I've enjoyed seeing the town come alive with activity once winter finally released its icy grip on the world. Storefronts have their welcome signs out on the clear sidewalks, and fresh flowers bloom all along the town green. People are walking around the neighborhood more and are even friendlier than they have been.

Today's an exciting day for the town as it's the annual Bramblewood Day. It's a day for all the local shops and vendors to display their goods at the town square under tents to avoid the direct sunlight beaming down on everyone. The event also hosts multiple food trucks and kid-friendly activities and rides. It's like a miniature carnival, and I didn't know this existed until I happened upon a flyer while Ben and I were browsing the shops the other weekend. We walked over from our apartment and sampled some snacks from the food trucks while browsing the vendor tents.

I'm looking at a painting of a naked woman being embraced by a demon with black wings. I'm not sure where Ben went, but as I am about to ask the shop owner about the price, someone calls my name. Turning around, I come face to face with the last person I want to see.

"Emily, I thought that was you." Logan smiles at me warmly, like he has never been happier to see me. He moves to give me a hug, and I stand there in shock as his arms wrap around me. He pulls away after an awkward second but keeps his hands on my arms as he looks down at me. "It's so good to see you."

"Hey, Logan," I clear my throat and step back so he would release me. "What are you doing here?"

He raises a brow at me as if I asked a rhetorical question. "I work for the town, remember?"

How could I have forgotten that Logan is the town's cop? I'd never run into him before when he was working, and since he's not in his uniform, it must be his day off.

"Oh, sorry, I forgot about that."

"How have you been?" He questions, eyes darting around, searching to see if I came alone. "You look great."

"Thanks..." My voice trails off, but Logan appears distracted. "You haven't been responding to any of my messages lately." He glares, his voice growing harder.

I frown in confusion. His abrupt change in demeanor is giving me whiplash.

"Are you still living with that guy? Ben?" Logan continues. I try to answer, but he cuts me off. "He's bad news. You need to be careful."

"What are you talking about?"

"I know you don't want to hear this, but... I have reason to believe that Ben isn't who you think he is."

I freeze.

"Excuse me?"

I watch with trepidation as Logan pulls out a folded piece of paper from his pocket and hands it to me. My hands tremble as I reach for it and unfold it with shaking fingers.

Subject: Benjamin Walker
Incident Report: Class D Misdemeanor — theft
Status: Unresolved Investigation

My chest tightens, and my eyes blur. It looks like a police report.

"You ran a background check on him?" My voice comes out shaky.

Logan moves closer, his voice low and worried. Repulsion floods me as his hand touches my shoulder, and I resist the impulse to recoil.

"I'm sorry, Emily. I thought you'd want to know what type of person you're with. I would never forgive myself if something happened to you."

Something doesn't feel right. This whole situation feels like a setup. My gut twists as I try to make sense of what's happening.

"Ben would never hurt me. He would never do anything to hurt me." It's the one thing I know beyond a shadow of a doubt. "You should go."

A look of shock washes over Logan's face as his expression falters. "I'm just trying to protect you."

"I don't need your protection. Not anymore."

I look at Logan—really look at him. His expression hardens under the scrutiny, dropping the mask of concern. It was all an act to get me to distrust Ben. This was never about protecting me. This was about asserting his control over me, making me doubt my relationship, and keeping me in the past, where I used to see Logan as my protector.

I crumple up the paper and shove it into his chest. His hand comes up in surprise and briefly grips mine before I pull away in disgust.

"You need to stop, Logan. Lose my number and stop texting me. We're over." I glare at him, hoping he gets the picture and leaves me alone.

"Is there a problem here?" I stiffen at the sound of Ben's gruff voice. At the feel of Ben's arms around my waist, I breathe a sigh of relief. I'm warmed by his heat at my back, dispelling the chill Logan's news has caused. Ben places a possessive kiss on my throat, and I turn my head slightly to him.

"Hey, you, there you are," I say to Ben, relief evident in my voice. "Logan was just leaving." I glare at Logan.

"Sorry, babe, I saw something I thought you'd like." He shows me a shopping bag. My attention catches on the unexpected gift. I squeal in excitement and try to grab the bag, but Ben pulls it away from me.

"Uh uh uh. Not yet," he tuts at me, and I pout like a toddler being deprived of a gift. Ben chuckles and pecks my nose with a sweet kiss, and we hear the clearing of a throat. We both look over to see a peeved Logan standing with his arms crossed.

"Oh. Sorry, forgot you were still here," Ben deadpans.

"I can see that. So, you two are together?" A look of anger twisted Logan's features.

"Yup," Ben replies curtly and steers me away with an arm around my shoulders. "Nice seeing you, Chad," he shouts over his shoulder, and we walk away. I glance behind me, catching sight of Logan standing rigidly, his eyes narrowed in a furious glare burning into our backs as we walk away.

I shake off the unsettling encounter and snuggle in closer to Ben. Forcing my mind to focus on the present.

"So, when can I see what you got me?" I whine.

"Soon." Ben smiles down at me.

We walk back to the apartment with me tucked under Ben's arm, and the mystery present swinging in his other hand. He won't let me open the present until after he makes me come twice. Only when we've come up for air, and the encounter with Logan is long forgotten, does he finally hand over the bag. I shriek in delight as I pull out the hand-wrapped miniature figurines of a pair of cats that resemble Buffy and Spike.

I thank him by jumping into his lap and giving him a kiss.

Sometimes, I feel like all of this is too good to be true, but rather than dwell on it, I feel grateful for what life has put us through to bring us together.

♥ ♥ ♥ ♥

The next day, I couldn't shake the unsettling feeling of my encounter with Logan. I couldn't escape his words in my mind the entire night. The strange encounter followed me in my sleep and haunted my dreams. The police report and Logan's constant texts have left me feeling uneasy. I haven't told Ben what's bothering me, even though he knows something is wrong.

I'm full of unanswered questions. I built up the nerve to talk to Ben about what happened with Logan, going over it repeatedly in my head, but he was over at Jason and Amanda's. Jason needed a hand to build something down in the basement. Ben invited me to hang out with Amanda, but my anxiety was too overwhelming.

I've cleaned every surface in the apartment until it sparkles. Even the cats are avoiding me after I used the vacuum cleaner for the third time. My furious pacing fails to alleviate my restlessness. As a car nears, I run to the window, a sharp exhale escaping me at the sight of Ben's car.

Finally, he's home.

Seconds tick by as I wait on the edge of the couch. In the hushed apartment, the sound of his keys unlocking the door is amplified. When he yells his usual greeting, letting me know he's home, my heart flutters excitedly. I'm overwhelmed by a sickening mix of anxiety and excitement. I'm so incredibly stimulated that I feel like I'm going to burst.

I remain still, my hands clasped, as he approaches. He

catches sight of me on the couch as he gets to the landing. A worried look replaces his smile, and he runs to me.

"What's wrong? What happened?"

I shake my head. "Nothing happened."

"Tell me what's wrong."

Exhaling deeply, I recount my conversation with Logan, omitting nothing. I cautiously bring up Logan's police report, noticing his expression harden into apathy. Feeling like ages have passed, I stop and sink into my seat. Letting everything go felt good.

Ben has been quietly and attentively listening to me. He seemed furious at first about what Logan said, but now it feels like he is concealing his true feelings.

"Ben?" My voice cracks as I wring my hands.

For a moment, he examines my face before collapsing onto the couch, throwing his head back with laughter.

His reaction baffles me.

"Ben? What's going on?" It feels like I'm not in on whatever the joke was.

Ben rubs his face, his laughter fading to a quiet chuckle. Turning his head, he looks at me and takes my hand.

"Your ex is a prick." I nod in agreement, waiting for Ben to continue. "When I was in college, I was arrested."

Shocked, I gasp, and he signals for me to let him continue.

"Now, before you freak out, it wasn't as big of a deal as he's making it out to seem. Jason and I were living in the dorms, and some frat boys were handing out T-shirts. Unfortunately, we found out later when the campus cops came knocking on our doors that the shirts had been stolen from the locker room. They wanted us to rat out who gave us the shirts, and we kept our mouths shut. That's where the misdemeanor comes from."

"Oh." I slump into his side. "That's it?"

"Yes, that's it." He chuckles as if the memory is still fresh in his mind.

"Yeah. Logan is a prick."

The absurdity of the situation makes me laugh. I can't believe I let Logan get under my skin again. He's done enough damage to my life. Never again, I vow.

32

Emily

"I think I'm dying," I pant as I collapse on the floor of the gym. The workout of the day included multiple rounds of burpees and lunges with some lightweight lifting exercises. While I don't mind weightlifting, I loathe burpees and lunges with a passion. I'm not surprised that the workout kicked my ass, but I have never felt this sick after a brutal workout before.

"You okay?" Maggie asks as she sits down next to me and sips her water. She hands me my protein shake, and I sit up to take a sip before lying back down on the ground.

"I feel like shit." Panting heavily, I can't seem to catch my breath, and the room feels like it's spinning. "I'll just lay here until I die."

Maggie laughs at my antics, and we catch up on work gossip. The mood shifts, a palpable tension hanging in the air, and I brace myself for what she's about to say.

"Have you heard from Logan since 'the incident'?" Maggie frowns.

The memory of my ex makes my skin crawl with revulsion.

"No, thank God. He's stopped texting me finally. It's almost like he's disappeared."

My breaths have returned to normal, and the racing in my chest has subsided. The dizziness has diminished, but the mention of Logan makes me queasy. When I finally peel myself off the ground, I feel a little better.

"I still can't believe he confronted you like that. And in public!"

"Yeah, me neither. It doesn't make any sense."

"It's almost like he hates seeing that you're happy and don't need him anymore."

"I never thought of it like that before."

Lost in thought, my brows knit together. Was Logan trying to manipulate me by making me doubt Ben's character? A few months ago, my loyalty to Logan clouded my judgment. I never would have thought Logan could be so deceitful, but now, away from his spell, his dishonesty is shockingly clear. The coldness in his eyes, the hollow ring to his voice. These things were always there. I just couldn't see them before.

"Well, I'm glad he's finally out of the picture, so you can move on with your life. He's been such a deadweight," Maggie continues. "You ready to get outta here?"

I nod and drag myself to standing.

"Ugh, I think I gained some weight." The swelling around my midsection is causing me a lot of discomfort; it feels distended. My clothes have been feeling snug, and I feel uncomfortable in my body.

"I don't know how that's possible. You work out all the time!" Megan replies, then adds, "Maybe you're just bloated. I always get bloated when it's time for my period."

I nod as I try to remember the last time I had my period. It's usually pretty regular, so I never keep track of it, but I should have had it a few weeks ago. I try not to let the rising panic take hold as we grab our things and head out. We usually grab breakfast at the local diner once a month, but I suddenly feel anxious and queasy.

"I'm gonna pass on breakfast, but I'll see you at work tomorrow!" We hug and say our goodbyes as I jump in the car. I try not to speed as I head to the nearest convenience store. Once inside the store, I casually walk to the pharmacy area, where the pregnancy tests are lined up on the shelves. There are so many options, but I go for the digital one that will clearly tell me if I'm being over dramatic or not.

The cashier checks me out, and as she's bagging the test along with some snacks I added last-minute, she tells me, "Good luck, and I hope you get the answer you want!"

I grab the bag she hands me and stroll out of the store. What answer do I want? I'm thirty years old, but am I ready for kids? How do I tell Ben? A million thoughts run through my mind as I drive back to the apartment.

I'm so worked up by the time I get home that I can't even pee on the damn stick. I grab a bottle of water from the pantry and chug it before hopping into the shower. I work through different scenarios as I wash my long hair. The lavender scent of the shampoo is soothing and helps me center myself. By the time I'm washing out the conditioner in my hair, I've decided that no matter the test results, I know I can handle it.

That we can handle it. Together.

Grabbing a towel and drying off, I wrap it around my body and finally plop on the toilet seat. After verifying the instructions, I pee on the stick and carefully replace the cap as I set an alarm for the mandatory two minutes. I finish drying off and get dressed so I don't sit and glare at the test. I'm sure that will somehow alter the results.

I'm fully dressed by the time my alarm goes off. I turn it off with a swipe and take a deep breath to center myself. Rolling my neck and shaking out my arms, I finally gain the courage to pick up the stick.

PREGNANT

The test result is self-explanatory, but I still stare at it in shock.

"Fuck."

♡ ♡ ♡ ♡ ♡

I bring the test back to my room and set it on the dresser. My thoughts swirling, I crawl into bed. My earlier confidence crumbled when faced with the stark reality of the positive test result. An icy wave of fear and uncertainty washes over me, the remnants of my bravado gone as quickly as the hot steam dissipating in my shower, leaving only a damp, chilling emptiness. I was drowning in a sea of possibilities, grasping for any lifeline.

The sound of the front door opening alerts me to Ben's arrival. I'm startled awake, my face wet with drool that I quickly swipe away as I leap from the bed. I must have fallen asleep at some point. Ben enters the room just as I find the test where I left it and shove it into my dresser. I turn around to greet his warm smile, and he reaches his arms out for a hug. I collapse into his embrace and let him hug me.

With him here, a sense of peace washes over me. I breathe deeply, the scent of his cologne filling my lungs and calming my anxieties.

"What's wrong?" he asks softly into my hair and squeezes me gently. I shake my head and bury my nose in his chest.

"I just missed you." It's not a lie.

He cups the back of my head and plants a kiss before pulling back to look at me. His eyes are sharp as he takes in my expression and tilts his chin down in a nod. He grabs my hand and pulls me into the kitchen. "Come eat dinner. I picked up your favorite Thai food."

My stomach gurgles in hunger. He sits me down and sets the

food in front of me. Suddenly, my favorite food doesn't seem so appetizing when all the scents hit me at once. Gagging, I cover my mouth with a hand and rush into the bathroom, but the wave of nausea dissipates by the time I make it there.

"Are you going to tell me what's wrong now?" Ben asks from the doorway, where he's leaning with his arms and ankles crossed. His perceptive eyes, sharp and knowing, saw right through me. I couldn't hide the truth from him, even if I wanted to.

"Yeah, I think we need to talk." The words were reminiscent of what he had told me just a month ago. I gesture for him to leave so I can slowly wash my hands and trudge out of the bathroom. I head to my room, grab the test, and meet him in our living room. Ben's sitting on the couch and has turned on Netflix. I edge my way into the room and sit on the edge of the loveseat so we're facing each other. He puts the remote down and turns his full attention to me, cocking an eyebrow.

Without saying a word, I pass the test to him and sit on my hands as soon as he grabs it. He looks at it for a brief second, with confusion marring his handsome face, before the meaning of the test clicks. His shocked face looks up and meets my gaze, but I can't tell what he's thinking by the expression.

Is he happy? Is he mad? Where do we go from here?

"Does this mean what I think it means?" he asks me slowly, like he's scared to believe the answer. I nod.

"I'm pregnant," I finally say and brace myself for his response. I expect him to explode with questions and disbelief. It's how I reacted, after all, but he surprises me when he jumps to his feet and picks me up. He hugs me tightly, and I hesitantly wrap my arms around him. I sag against his body and release all the tension that I've felt until this moment.

He sits down and cradles me in his lap.

"How are you feeling?" he murmurs into my hair.

"I don't know. I felt fine until today, but I guess I've been more tired than usual. I just thought... you know... we've been very busy and not sleeping a lot." I nuzzle into his neck, breathing in the familiar scent of his cologne and the warmth of his skin.

"I'm guessing the Thai food was a bad idea." He chuckles softly, and his hand rubs my back in soothing circles.

"That was very nice of you, and I'm sorry for the way I reacted."

"More for me." I can hear the grin in his words. He pulls me back to look me in the eye. "Are you okay?" he asks me with genuine concern.

"I'm scared," I admit in a low whisper.

He nods sagely, like he knew what my answer was before I even said it out loud. "I am too but we'll be okay, tiger. I promise."

"You're not upset?"

"Upset? No. I mean, we've been having a lot of sex, so this was bound to happen." He grins triumphantly, and I swat at his chest. A chuckle escapes his lips, but his face quickly turns serious, the smile fading. "It's scary to think that we could be parents soon if that's what we decide to do."

"I must have missed a couple of my birth control pills. I don't know how else this could have happened."

He pulls me back into his chest and tucks me into his neck as he continues to rub my back. After a few moments, he sets me down and disappears into the kitchen. I grab the remote and pick a show we both enjoy. Ben returns with a plate of buttered toast and bottled water for me.

"Eat something, and then we can talk." He leaves the items and goes back for his Thai food before joining me on the couch. We eat in silence, and it's not as awkward as I thought it would be. He seems to take this much better than I imagined, too. With the toast finished, I'm ready to tackle the drunken noodles he picked up for me. I eat half of it before calling it quits. I let Ben clean up after us as I settle into the couch and brace myself for the upcoming conversation.

Ben comes back and sits down next to me. He picks up my legs and places them across his lap in a familiar move. He finds my blanket and places it on my lap, and then he's rubbing gentle circles on my legs that make me moan in pleasure.

"This is how we ended up in this situation." He smiles sweetly at me.

"Yeah, I guess you're right."

"What do you want to do?" he asks me quietly. I pause before answering in a rush.

"I want to keep it." I look up at him through my lashes and see him nodding as if in agreement.

"Okay."

"Okay...?"

"Yes. Okay." He grabs my hand and squeezes it.

"It's still very early, so I need to call the doctor..." I trail off as my mind spins with what I'm supposed to do next.

"We'll figure it out together, tiger." He kisses my hand, and my worries are at ease.

That night, we slept curled around each other. I wasn't feeling up to fooling around, and Ben seemed content to follow my lead.

I can't believe I'm pregnant.

33

Ben

PREGNANT???

I'm going to be a father. I am going to be… a father.

The phrase plays on repeat in my mind as I lay in the dark. Emily is snoring softly beside me, but I've been restless since she showed me the test results. At first, I didn't believe what I was seeing. I didn't think Emily was pranking me, but it seemed impossible at first.

It's still surreal we're expecting a baby. I knew having kids was in my future, but I could never picture it happening when Melissa and I were together. Emily's pregnancy announcement scared me at first. Of course, it did. It is a natural reaction to unexpected news. Though I'm not surprised she got pregnant so quickly since we've been fucking like cats in heat, she had been on birth control. I knew oral contraceptives were not completely reliable, but the chances of it failing were still low.

One thing is obvious: I can see a future with Emily in it. I can't even imagine a life without her in it.

I'm going to be a father.

It seems absolutely absurd. How am I expected to take care of another person when I am barely holding myself together? Not to mention, a significant promotion is on the horizon, requiring overseas travel to manage our international sites. With a baby coming, I need to rethink my priorities.

And Emily? I know what I feel about her is more than just lust, but our relationship is still new. We're still getting to know each other. Can we handle bringing on a baby right now?

One thing I know for certain is that whatever Emily decides, I will fully support her. If she decides to keep the baby, I will move heaven and earth to make it possible. We'll probably need more space when the baby gets here. There are so many things we'll have to consider if that's what she decides.

And if she decides not to keep the baby? It would be a decision I know she wouldn't make lightly. Even if the thought hurts, I'll fully support her in her decision.

I'm going to be a father!

Thinking about it makes me even more sure I can be a great dad. Seeing Jason with his baby made me wonder what it would look like when my time came. Of course, I didn't think it would happen as soon as it did, but the idea didn't scare me as much as I thought it would.

I should probably feel more fear and anxiety than I do, but I suspect the woman by my side has something to do with alleviating my concerns. The thought of watching her swell with my child growing inside her fills me with pride. It's primitive, but I can't help it. Men are simple creatures, after all.

If anything, the idea turns me on so much I've been lying here with my cock at half-mast the entire time. Emily passed out almost as soon as her head hit the pillow. I don't blame her. She's trying to grow another human inside of her. My child.

I put a baby in her belly.

I think about what our future might look like with a child in the picture. I want to be able to provide everything they both will need. We'll probably outgrow the apartment quickly, and the housing market is improving. It might be one of the best times to buy a new house for the first time in almost a decade.

I know we're doing things out of order, but eventually, we'll have to discuss marriage.

My cock hardens at the thought of calling Emily my wife. My wife. Nothing sounds sweeter than the sound of calling her my wife.

The timeline is much faster than either of us expected, but it feels right.

The thought of marrying Emily feels right. It makes sense. We make sense. My heart swells, overflowing with the promise of our life together.

Everything happens for a reason, and sometimes you have to make mistakes. It's too bad it was an expensive mistake. Next time, the ring I buy will be for just one person, and she's right here with me.

I turn on my side and prop my head on my fist. Looking down at Emily's sleeping form, her face relaxed in sleep, lips parted slightly as she snores. I can't help the squeezing in my chest at the idea of spending the rest of our lives together.

She's the one, as cliche as it sounds. I'd known for a while but have been ignoring it until now. There's no use denying it anymore.

Life is about to change for us both.

34
Emily

Based on my missed period, the doctor had estimated that I was about seven weeks pregnant when I called them the following day. It was too soon for them to see me, so they had me make an appointment at the nine-week mark. Between then and now, I've taken several more tests which showed the same results. I guess I won't really believe it's happening until I hear that heartbeat or see the little bean on the ultrasound.

I told Ben when my appointment was, and since it was during the work week, I didn't expect him to come, but he shocked me and took the day off so he could be at my side. He must have seen the shock on my face when he told me he was coming with me. He kissed me on my forehead and said sweetly, "We're in this together, tiger."

While a part of me knew it wasn't like Ben to let me handle things on my own, another more jaded part of me expected to only rely on myself to get through this life-changing moment. The thought of never being alone again brings tears to my eyes. My pregnancy hormones are making me emotional.

That's how I ended up in my obstetrician's office, wearing only a flimsy gown I'd been told to put on like a bathrobe. The table is cold underneath me as we wait for the ultrasound technician to return. Ben's sitting in the chair next to me, lending me his quiet strength as we wait anxiously. I know he's nervous by the bouncing of his knee.

A knock precedes the entry of an older woman who introduces herself as the technician. She goes over the procedure so we know what to expect. She instructs me to lie back as she turns on her machine and dons a pair of medical gloves.

"Sorry, this may feel cold." I try not to flinch at the coolness, and the next thing I know, she's placing the wand over the goo. After a few sweeps, she finds what she's looking for; then, with some clicking of the buttons on the ultrasound machine, the rapid rhythm of a heartbeat floods the room.

Ben's hand clenches in mine as we stare at each other in awe. Tears well up in his eyes as we listen to the sound of the baby's heartbeat fill the room—our baby. I smile at him, and he places a chaste kiss on my lips. The ultrasound technician takes a few pictures and prints out a handful for us. She informs us that the doctor will have to go over the results with us as she cleans up her mess.

"Congratulations!" she shouts before waltzing out the door.

The doctor comes in shortly after. She's in her mid-fifties and has a warm smile on her face. As she sits down on her stool, she introduces herself and informs us I'm measuring to be about nine weeks along. The estimated due date would be around the end of February. She explains that she'll be ordering some bloodwork, and then she's gone before I can even think of questions to ask her.

Ben helps me get dressed, and we walk out hand in hand to the receptionist to book my next appointment. It isn't until we're both in the car that we turn to look at each other and hug.

"We're having a baby!" Ben cups my face with his warm palm and stares at me with so much warmth and affection in his eyes it makes my heart hurt.

"We're having a baby," he echoes, then kisses me gently.

We make love later that night. Our movements, which are usually frantic and desperate, with both of us eager to touch one another, are slower and more reverent tonight as if we have all the time in the world. It feels like he's worshipping my body and the miracle we made together. If I had any more doubts about how Ben feels about this unexpected pregnancy, he washes away my worries with each caress of his gentle hands and the soft kisses he showers me with.

35

Emily

The rest of the first trimester drags by. I am crippled with intense fatigue and morning sickness that persists all day long. I want to beat whoever coined the term "morning sickness" with a bat until they're a bloody pulp. Morning sickness gives me the illusion of hope that I will feel better as the day progresses. It should not send me running to the bathroom dry heaving at random times throughout the day. My appetite has been nonexistent, thanks to the ever-present nausea and dry heaves. The bright side? I haven't actually lost any of my meals yet.

The fatigue is on a whole other level. Most nights, I am in bed and knocked out before the clock has struck 9 p.m. I don't wake until the alarm blares its horn the next day. I drag my exhausted self through my morning routine, and work feels like torture. I count the minutes until I can go back to bed again. On my days off, I sleep in until mid-morning.

I have little energy most days, and my workouts have been pathetic, but I feel optimistic that things will get better soon. At least, that's what everyone keeps telling me about how wonderful the second trimester will be. I haven't started showing yet, but I feel bloated and disgusting. I have so much more respect for pregnant women now that I'm going through it myself.

Ben and I have been spending our evenings researching what to expect when adding another person to our still very new relationship. He doesn't seem worried about our future, but I am riddled with anxiety about what comes next. I have yet to meet his parents, and I know he hasn't told them much about our unexpected news. From what he's told me about them, they seem like nice people. We have dinner plans with them this weekend, and I'm queasy just thinking about it.

Meeting Ben's parents will also serve the purpose of letting them know that they'll also be grandparents. It makes me wonder how I should handle telling my parents. I haven't seen or talked to them in years. My father and I get along fine, but he's a passenger in the relationship while my mother is the driver. She's the reason for many of my childhood traumas that have echoed into my adult life.

My mother met my father when she was just a teenager. My grandmother had fled her home country with her six kids and the clothes on their backs in search of a better life—the all-American dream of better opportunities and freedom from an oppressive government regime. Upon entering the country, they stayed with family members and had to travel every few months. It was on one of those trips that my parents met.

My father was also staying with family in the country, though he had to leave his elderly parents behind. My parents' story was defined by necessity, not love. At the tender age of seventeen, my mother became pregnant with me, and I was born shortly before her eighteenth birthday. Unfortunately, my mother found out after she had me and, while pregnant with my sister, that my father was previously married and had children he did not bring to America.

While I can understand the devastation my mother must have felt to find out her husband and father of her children had a secret family, I was also tired of her using me as a verbal, emotional, and, sometimes, physical punching bag. After many years of her abuse, I finally had to learn to set some boundaries, which meant walking away from my mother and, ultimately, my father. I don't hold the same level of resentment for my father as I do for my mother, but I also can't forgive him for turning a blind eye to the abuse for so many years.

The last time I spoke to my mother, I told her I could not continue talking to her or be near her if she wouldn't stop mistreating me. It was one of the hardest things I had ever done until this point. I've learned to be alone and depend only on myself for everything. Through the separation from my parents, I have become hyper-independent to the point of feeling like I don't need anyone in my life. I haven't thought about it much until now, but it possibly contributed to why my relationships fail.

How can you be in a relationship with someone who doesn't really even need you for anything? I'm sure it would impact self-esteem or egos. I guess I'll have to find a therapist to work through these issues. Ben nudges me with his knee as if he could sense my racing thoughts.

"Penny for your thoughts?" he murmurs softly, and our eyes meet. He reaches a hand to brush back a stray hair and tuck it behind my ears. I turn my face into the palm of his hand and let his touch center me. After a moment, I pull away and heave a dramatic sigh.

"I guess we should probably talk about my parents." He looks at me curiously but says nothing. I tell him the whole sad story of my childhood. He listens with a contemplative look but doesn't interrupt me. Finally, when I'm done with the verbal diarrhea, I plop on my back on the couch and cover my face with my hands.

"Ugh. I just don't know what to do. Should I tell them? Do they want to know? Would they even care? It's been almost ten years," I lament while Ben picks up my feet and places them in his lap, rubbing small circles around the arch of my feet. The foot massage makes me moan in pleasure, and I feel his body tense. It's been a few days since we've had sex since I've been passing out as soon as my head hits the pillow lately.

"Do you want to know what I think?" He poses the question, but I know it's rhetorical. "I think you should tell them if you want to. They don't need to be involved in anything you don't want them to be. Whatever you decide, we'll do it together."

These damn pregnancy hormones keep wreaking havoc on my emotions as his words bring tears to my eyes. I sniff and crane my neck to look up at him and mouth the words, "Thank you."

I must have fallen asleep on the couch at some point. I stir awake when Ben lifts me and cradles me to his chest to carry me into our bedroom. He tucks me in, and I fall asleep surrounded by his warmth.

36
Emily

The second trimester arrives like a breath of fresh air, lifting the fog from my brain. I feel more like myself again, and it's amazing how much more I can accomplish when I'm not weighed down by severe fatigue and morning-not-morning sickness. I've put on some weight, but otherwise, I haven't started showing yet. We won't find out the gender for quite a few more weeks, but Ben and I have bets on whether it's a boy or a girl. My money is on a girl, while Ben is confident it's a boy. The thought of having a penis growing inside of me makes me feel weird, so I'm hoping I'm right.

The weeks pass by in a blur of excitement as Ben and I prepare for a gender reveal party. When I officially hit twelve weeks, I felt more comfortable sharing the news with people. I was riddled with nerves when we met Ben's parents for dinner a few weeks ago. Once dinner was served, Ben grabbed my hand under the table and told his parents that we were having a baby. His parents' initial shock gave way to joy and excitement over the news, calming my nerves. His mom started crying and gave me a big hug at the end of the night. I didn't realize I wanted his parents' approval until that moment, and it made me wish I had a better relationship with my parents.

Later that night, while we were lying in bed after Ben fucked me into oblivion, I told him I wanted to at least tell my parents about the baby. We can figure out the details later, but I felt it was necessary to tell them for my peace of mind. Ben had placed a soft kiss at my temple and held me until I fell asleep.

♡ ♡ ♡ ♡ ♡

"I t's going to be fine. You'll see," Ben reassures me and squeezes my hand as he pulls into the parking lot of the local Vietnamese restaurant in town. It's one of my favorite restaurants, and it serves authentic Vietnamese cuisine. I haven't been here in a few months, but the thought of having some of my favorite foods makes me feel excited, even though the reason we're here in the first place is to meet my parents face-to-face. It's been about a decade since I last saw them in person, but when I reached out to my mom and asked her if she wanted to grab lunch with Ben and me, she responded promptly.

We approach the restaurant, and Ben holds the door open for me. He places a hand on the small of my back as we walk inside. I glance around and see my parents seated halfway across the small restaurant. My dad perks up when he sees me, and my mom looks over her shoulder. She offers a small smile, which surprises me. I didn't know how she would react to seeing me again after so long. It wasn't like we left things on good terms.

My parents stand up as we approach the table. I stand there awkwardly until Ben breaks the silence and introduces himself to my parents. He shakes hands with my father and pulls out my chair for me. We aren't sitting for long before the server comes over to hand us some more menus.

I take the time to look over the menu even though I always order the same thing every time I come here. Figuring out how to tell them about the pregnancy requires time. I also don't know how they'd take the fact that I am having a baby with a man who is clearly not Vietnamese. Although I don't believe my parents are prejudiced, I know they'd prefer I marry within our culture.

Raised with most of my family under the same roof, we were taught the importance of cultural heritage. To my grandmother, preserving our family's legacy was paramount. As children, our mother told my sister and me that we needed to marry within our Vietnamese community. Yet, here I am, sitting next to my Caucasian boyfriend. Expecting a baby. Unmarried.

My heart is pounding so hard I'm shocked others don't notice. While I don't regret my decisions, it's tough to deal with my parents' disapproval.

I don't realize I'm fidgeting until Ben grabs my hand and places it on his thigh. He keeps his warm hand on mine. The comforting touch centers me and eases some of my nerves.

"So, how are you doing?" my mom finally breaks the silence in her heavily accented English.

"Um, I'm fine. How are you?" I look up at my mom but don't make eye contact, as it can be mistaken as a sign of disrespect in our culture.

"Good. I've been good." My mom nods adamantly. She opens her mouth to say something, but the server returns for our order. I reach into my purse to pull out the ultrasound picture I had framed and look at Ben, who gives me a small nod.

"So, um, we have some news," I say nervously before reaching across the table to hand my mom the picture frame. She looks confused for a second as she takes it from me and looks down at the black-and-white photo. My dad looks over curiously at what I handed over to my mom.

It takes her a few seconds, but she gasps when she realizes what she's seeing. When she looks up at me, I see she has tears in her eyes. My dad still looks confused, so I tell him Ben and I are having a baby. At the news, my dad glances at me, and I see tears filling his eyes, too.

I squirm in my seat at the show of emotions from my estranged parents. To be honest, I'm surprised at how well it's going. I expected disappointment or a mean retort from my mom, but that hasn't happened.

"I'm so happy for you," my mom finally says after a few more seconds. She gets up and tries to hug me while I'm sitting, and I try to give her an awkward one-armed hug.

"Thank you," I say, my voice husky from unshed tears.

Once she's seated again, we exchange glances, relaxing visibly as a sense of relief washes over us. The rest of the meal goes off without a hitch, and when we get ready to leave, my mom pulls me into a big hug. I'm so surprised by the show of affection and glance at Ben helplessly. I must look as confused as I feel, and he laughs at me—the jerk.

When she finally lets me go, we walk out together and say our goodbyes. Ben holds my hand and opens the car door for me. I take a deep breath as he makes his way around to the driver's side and gets in. As soon as the door shuts, he turns his body to face me.

"Come here." He grabs me, giving me a tight hug, and I burst into tears. He hushes me as I let it all out. After a couple of minutes, I finally lift my head and wipe my tears away. I blame it on the pregnancy hormones.

I never realized how much my parents' absence in my life had impacted me until now. Hope fills me when I think of our future. I'm not naïve enough to believe that everything will be perfect, but the woman who sat across from me today was a completely different person than the one I knew growing up. I could tell by her demeanor and the aura she exuded. She looked happy and healthy, as if she no longer had this heavy weight dragging her down.

"I guess I needed that. Thank you." Ben wipes an errant tear from my cheek and kisses my lips softly before pulling away. He rests his forehead against mine and looks into my eyes for a few seconds, and we soak in the moment.

37

Emily

I wish I could say that the rest of my pregnancy went well, but just as I was getting used to feeling like myself again, I hit a major setback. I was ecstatic when I started showing around sixteen weeks. While caring for a patient, I first felt the baby kicking at eighteen weeks. At first, I thought it was gas bubbles, but it felt like butterflies were tickling me on the inside. Once I realized what the sensation was, I ran to the main desk to tell my unit secretary, Eloise, the news. She was as excited as I was and gave me a quick hug before I went back to work.

Eloise is the unit's grandmother. She was kind and welcoming to me when I first joined the team. She cried when I told her I was pregnant and made sure I didn't do any heavy lifting. Unfortunately, heavy lifting is unavoidable with the type of patients that we care for. It often includes turning and repositioning patients who are medication-induced comas while their bodies need time to heal from trauma.

My last checkup was yesterday morning. I'm just a little over twenty-four weeks along, and though I am measuring small, the doctor seems happy with my progress. I was recently diagnosed with gestational diabetes, much to my dismay. I'm not thrilled about the restricted diet, but I am doing my best to keep my blood sugar levels in the normal range. However, I sometimes experience unexplained high blood sugar levels.

I also mentioned that I am having increased pain in my groin. The pain is most intense when walking or moving. The doctor told me it's normal to feel pubic pain and chalked it up to me being petite. He left the exam room before I could ask any follow-up questions. His nonchalant response to my worry left a bitter taste in my mouth, but I convinced myself it was just my anxiety talking.

Today started off just like any other shift. I had to transport a sedated patient down to the imaging department, along with an entire team of other medical professionals. The patient required a ventilator to breathe, so it was all hands on deck. I took my lunch break, but I also had to make sure to eat throughout my shift. After a long shift at the hospital, I'm ready to put my feet up and rest. They aren't swollen yet, but they need attention. Maybe Ben will massage them for me when he gets back.

Thoughts of how sweet Ben has been causes a small smile to spread across my face while a warm feeling spreads through me. He shows his love by taking care of me. I know he feels power-less as my body undergoes these significant transformations to grow our child. Pregnancy is both an amazing and terrifying experience.

Lately, our sex life has picked up, but he doesn't pressure me into sex if I'm not feeling it. It hadn't occurred to me how frequently Logan used guilt to coerce me into sleeping with him. Ben helped me realize that many of Logan's seemingly harmless actions were actually emotionally manipulative. Being with Ben has helped me heal as I try to undo the damage that Logan caused. Logan's charm immediately drew me in, and I felt content. I know that I'm partly to blame for allowing it to happen.

When I get home, I change out of my scrubs and relax on the couch. Ben isn't home yet since he was at happy hour with some of his work buddies. He had invited me to join, but I declined. I haven't felt up to socializing much outside of work lately.

I'm not sure how long I stay on the couch, but it must have been at least a couple of hours. When I move to get up off the couch, I almost fall to the floor at the intense pain that shoots through my groin and radiates down my back. I figure my legs must have fallen asleep or something, but when I try to walk, the pain only intensifies. It feels like I am being ripped apart at the crotch with each step that I take.

The pain hurts so much that I end up crawling on my hands and knees the rest of the way to my bedroom, and it takes a great deal of effort to heave myself onto the bed. Once I lay down, it's almost impossible to get comfortable due to the pain. I swear I heard a popping noise earlier when I first got up off the couch, but I was half awake.

I must have fallen asleep because I wake up to Ben climbing into bed. He pulls me close to him so that he's nestled against my back. He kisses me on my temple and whispers goodnight. I fall back asleep with his arms wrapped around me.

I woke up in pain again this morning. I had hoped that the back and pelvic pain would have gotten better overnight, but I guess not. Getting ready is difficult for me, and I'm getting concerned. I don't remember being in this much pain before.

I'm due at work in an hour, and I worry about whether I'll be able to finish my shift today. I don't have any medicine besides prenatal vitamins in the apartment, so I ask Ben to pick up some Tylenol when he's out and about later.

When I'm at work, the pain only gets worse despite trying to rest as much as possible. I informed my charge nurse that I might need to take on a lighter assignment today since I'm not feeling so well. She gave me a patient who requires one-to-one supervision instead of our usual two-to-one ratio. I'm thankful, as that means I cut down the amount of walking I need to do between patients' rooms.

By the end of my shift, I feel the worse for wear. I call Ben on the way home and tell him what's going on. He meets me at the doorway and helps me walk up the stairs to our floor.

I don't think there's anything wrong with the baby since I've felt its kicks consistently throughout the day. I promise Ben that I'll call my doctor first thing in the morning, since the office is closed for the weekend.

The next day, the nurse returns my phone call, and she tells me that the pain I'm feeling is normal, but I know that something isn't right. I've taken the rest of the week off of work so I can rest, but it seems no amount of sleep helps. The pain is so intense that walking is excruciating. I can't imagine this pain persisting for the remainder of my pregnancy. I'm barely in the third trimester as it is.

I text Amanda to see if she has time to meet for lunch. She responds after a few minutes, and we decide on the new sandwich shop that just opened up down the street from the apartment.

We're seated in the window seat when she asks me how I'm feeling. I tell her what I've been feeling for the past couple of days. She informs me she had felt some pain in her groin, but it didn't happen until much later in her pregnancy. I'm relieved to know that the pain seems normal, but something still doesn't sit right with me. We spend some time catching up, and before long, I'm headed back to the apartment.

After a slow ascent up the winding stairs, I collapse on the couch and pull out my phone. I open my internet browser and search up 'groin pain during pregnancy.' I find some information about how pregnancy hormones can relax the joints and ligaments that are at the front of the pelvis to allow the baby to pass through the birth canal. The joints help with the movement of the pelvis and absorb shock during activities like walking or running. Ligaments hold the joints together to prevent them from moving unevenly or beyond what is comfortable. The process typically occurs later on in pregnancy.

I also find some interesting articles about a rare pregnancy-related disability called symphysis pubis dysfunction or SPD. It's a rare disorder, and the fundamental characteristic of SPD is pain or discomfort in the front of the pelvis. Pain can also go to the back of the pelvis. The pubic joints being prematurely unstable can cause the pelvis to feel loose.

Unfortunately, the commonality among the many articles I found is that certain movements can make the pain worse. These movements include walking, bending, going up and down the stairs, and getting in and out of bed or the car, essentially any movement that requires spreading your legs apart, thereby making the pelvis unstable.

I feel like a light bulb goes off. I'm both happy and disappointed to be able to put a name on what I've been feeling. It will make working a physically intensive job very difficult as my pregnancy progresses because of the increase in weight and pressure on the pelvic floor. Stopping work during my pregnancy wasn't something I expected. I want to work until the day I give birth, but it seems my body has other plans for me. I can't even articulate how frustrated and helpless this makes me feel. My choice is being taken away from me, and I'm a passenger in my body.

I put my phone aside and take a deep breath. While I'm relieved to know that what I'm likely feeling is not harmful to me or the baby, I wish there was a solution. What can I do other than rest and restrict activity? Only Tylenol is safe for pain relief during pregnancy, as most other pain medications are unsafe for the baby.

The bright side? The condition isn't permanent. All the articles agree that the pain could last until after the baby is born. I found links to purchase a support belt to help ease some of the pressure and weight off of the pelvis. After looking up some reviews, I purchase a pink-colored belt that will be delivered tomorrow.

Feeling accomplished that I have somewhat of a plan, I sit

back and try to think of the positives. I just have to make it a few more months before the baby is born.

❀ ❀ ❀ ❀ ❀

Ben comes home later that night to find me moping in bed. I tried to go to the grocery store to pick up a few items for dinner, but the pain was so excruciating. Every step I took was torture, and I barely held my tears back in the snack aisle. I abandoned my cart next to the chips and left. I didn't let the tears fall on the drive home. It took a great deal of effort to get up the stairs, and about halfway up, I sat down on the steps. I meant to rest for a few seconds but ended up climbing up the stairs on my butt. I'm thankful for the side rails because I don't know if I could have made it off the top step without it.

I finally let the tears fall when I made it into my bed, and I have been lying here ever since.

Here I am, pregnant and in a relationship with someone I never thought would be my other half until circumstances pushed us together. I should be happy and celebrating, but all I feel is a deep sense of sadness over not having a beautiful pregnancy. I feel lied to and cheated out of a magical experience so many other women enjoy.

I'm crying because I'm in so much pain. I couldn't even endure a quick trip to the grocery store. Every step feels like I'm being ripped apart. Even a simple action like turning over in bed sends sharp shards of pain through my groin and my back. I can't get comfortable. Walking hurts. Sitting hurts. Lying in bed hurts. Everything I do hurts. I can't even take pain relievers because I'm worried about hurting the baby. It's probably irrational, but I don't want to mess this up.

All I have is my poor attitude and a growing baby who, no

doubt, is feeling my sour mood. I'm having a pity party, but at least there are two of us attending. I would laugh at my joke if the circumstances weren't so sad. Buffy and Spike do their best to comfort me. Their purrs help soothe me, and I snatch Spike in a bear hug. He pretends he hates it, but I know Spike loves to snuggle.

The baby has been active throughout the day, and whenever I feel it kick, I smile. My hands gently touch my swollen belly. Gratitude mixes with an overwhelming desire to simply wallow in my feelings.

Ben finds me in my room with all the lights off. It's fall, and the daylight hours are getting shorter. I hear him creeping into the bedroom on cushioned feet and pulling back the covers as he climbs into bed with me.

He says nothing as he pulls me closer, and I sniffle into my pillow.

"Hey, tiger," he says softly against my temple, placing a kiss there. "How are you holding up?"

I take a moment to answer him, trying to compose myself so he can't tell that I've spent most of my day crying about my situation.

"I tried going to the grocery store, and I had to leave. It hurt so much." My voice cracks on the last word as a fresh round of tears flood my eyes. Despite my efforts to prevent them, they fall regardless. Sitting up, Ben grabbed the box of tissues I had on the nightstand table and handed me a couple. I murmur a thanks and wipe my tears away. Grimacing as I blow my nose at how sexy I must look right now.

When I've finally gotten myself back together again, Ben gently turns me around so that we're lying face-to-face. I don't meet his eyes, and he brings a hand under my chin and lifts my face until our eyes meet.

I expected his eyes to be filled with pity or remorse, but all I find is concern and warmth in his gaze.

"Tell me what's on your mind," he gently coaxes.

I sniffle and move to lay my head on his chest. At the sound of his heartbeat, I find mine has calmed down to match his rhythm.

"I have to work this weekend, and I don't know how I'm going to make it through a shift, much less three shifts back to back."

Instead of platitudes, Ben strokes my back in soothing circles.

"What do you want to do?"

I take a moment to answer him. All day long, it's been on my mind. I reached out to my doctor's office earlier to request another appointment. They finally called me back and said they could fit me in next Monday.

I take a deep breath, filling my lungs with Ben's unique scent that always calms me.

"I'm going to go in tomorrow and see how I feel," I decide. I know that it's probably not a good idea since I barely made it through to the grocery store today, but I have to try. I need to know what I'm capable of.

"I have an appointment on Monday." I pause before continuing, "I also canceled my gym membership for now."

I feel him rear back in shock. He knows how important it is for me to be active. Exercise has been helpful for my mood and often helps me deal with my depression.

"Are you sure that's a good idea?" he finally asks.

"Yeah. I mean, I can't do most of the workouts anymore, and now I can barely walk. I will go back after the baby is here."

I know I will have to return to the gym, and I dread how that will go. I'm sure that it will hurt a lot, considering it'll be months by the time I am cleared by the doctors to resume physical activity.

Instead of responding, Ben pulls me in closer and hugs me to his chest. I must fall asleep because Ben is shaking me awake to eat dinner. He helps me get out of bed and follows close behind me as I shuffle to the kitchen. Ben pulls out my chair for me, and I ease into the seat.

He sits across from me and clears his throat. "I'm going to take a half-day tomorrow," he mentions casually. "I can drive you to work on my way there and pick you up after."

Ben knows I have to park in the employee garage, which is a couple of blocks from the hospital. There are no shuttles to the building, and it's about a ten-minute walk to get to my unit. If he drops me off in front of the building, it will cut down my commute by seven minutes.

Every minute counts, and I'm not too proud to accept the help.

"I'll take you to your appointment on Monday," Ben continues. He's been to almost all of my doctor's appointments so far.

"You don't have to—"

"I want to go." His tone holds no room for argument.

"Okay," I say meekly, though inside, I'm preening at his attention.

As someone who has been independent for so long, it's nice to feel taken care of for once.

38

Ben

I took the day off today to take Emily to her appointment. She's a stubborn woman, and she's not used to being taken care of. My jaw clenches at the thought of her being alone for so many important things in her life. I'll make sure she will never be alone ever again.

Last weekend, I dropped her off at the main entrance of the hospital where she works. I barely restrained myself from getting out, scooping her up, and shoving her back in the car. I clenched the steering wheel so tight I thought it would break apart beneath my tight grip. It pained me to see her in so much distress. She tries to put on a brave front, but I can tell by the strain on her face that each step hurts her.

I only agreed to her going to work because I knew she wouldn't appreciate being told what to do. She needs to decide for herself what she is capable of doing. I've learned this about her over the short time we've been together.

She possesses a radiant spirit and a generous heart. She protects herself and keeps people at a distance. I've managed to penetrate her defenses and into her heart. It's a place I have no plans of leaving. I would be a fool to let a woman like her go.

I'm so incredibly blessed; the feeling of being worthy of her love and attention is beyond words. Every shared moment is a testament to her affection and trust. Our child will undoubtedly be raised in a home filled with love and care; I know this without a shadow of a doubt.

Now that I know what being in love feels like, I can't believe I ever tried to fool myself into believing Melissa and I were ever in love. We were friendly acquaintances who jumped into a relationship with no genuine connection. I never once felt my heart stop beating when she looked at me. Or felt the fire burning in my veins with the need to touch and consume her. The urge to be inside both her mind and body is overwhelming. I want to wrap myself around her heart and soul so we can never be separated.

Dr. Freedman's entrance interrupts my thoughts as she enters the exam room. She's an older woman who Emily and I have seen once before. Dr. Freedman has a team of rotating doctors so that Emily and I can meet everyone since we won't know who will be on-call when she goes into labor.

I get up and offer my hand to Dr. Freedman, which she takes firmly before turning her attention to Emily, who is seated in the chair and not on the exam table. I know it's because it hurts her too much to step up onto the stool. Since today's visit doesn't involve her needing to undress, she settles into the closest chair to the door.

"Hi, Emily. How are you?" Dr. Freedman asks softly.

I grab hold of Emily's hand and squeeze it reassuringly. I see her take in a deep breath before she tells Dr. Freedman what has been going on. She details her symptoms and summarizes the research she's been doing. I'm watching Dr. Freedman closely for any reaction, but the woman does not show any emotion on her face. I'm sure it has to do with her line of work.

"I'm having a lot of problems with working," Emily admits begrudgingly.

"What is it that you do for work?" Dr. Freedman asks gently.

"I'm a nurse and work in the trauma ICU."

Dr. Freedman nods in understanding. "Busy unit, I assume?" She doesn't wait for Emily to answer before stating with finality, "Emily, I'm placing you on bed rest until delivery. Unfortunately, your symptoms will only worsen the closer we get to when the baby arrives. The stress on your body and gestational diabetes might speed up the due date."

Emily sits in stunned silence. I'm not sure if she had expected this outcome, but I'm relieved to hear that she won't have to put herself in any unnecessary situations that cause her pain.

I clear my throat and ask some follow-up questions about what that might mean for Emily. Dr. Freedman suggests physical therapy and some safe pain relievers, though the most important thing is to rest.

Dr. Freedman turns to Emily and tells her she'll need to have some paperwork completed to take her out of work. Emily nods along, but I know she's still processing the news.

I guide her out of the office, and we grab lunch nearby. She's still quiet, and I watch her closely. After a few moments, she finally looks up from her salad and looks at me. She gives me a wane smile, and I reach across the table to hold her hand.

"I think we'll be okay," she finally says.

I nod in agreement because how can it not be?

"It's for the best. This way, you can spend more time finding us a new house or something." I wink at her and take a sip of my water.

"A house?" She widens her eyes at me comically.

"We're going to need more space with the baby coming."

"More space…"

"And you'll have more time to plan the gender reveal party."

I can see when her spirits lift again. Her back straightens, and I see the spark return to her eyes. The past few weeks had been agonizing to watch as her inner light had dimmed like a slow, painful decline. Like watching a candle burn down, each flicker and crackle was a painful reminder of her fading spirit. Never before have I felt this helpless.

"Oh my god, how could I have forgotten about the party!?"

"My family is very excited. They haven't heard of a gender reveal party before."

Her shoulders drop as she deflates, and my heart sinks at the sight.

"What's wrong?"

"I haven't asked my parents if they wanted to be there yet." She gives me a guilty look.

"Do you want them there?"

She considers my question while sipping on her seltzer water. I know she's buying herself more time to think.

"I know I want to give them another chance." Her words come out slowly. I nod encouragingly as our eyes meet across the table. I'm glad she can confide in me about her concerns.

"You know what I think?"

"What?" She tilts her head at me in question.

"You have a good heart, and they'd be stupid to not take this chance to see you again."

She blushes and looks down at the table. Her dark hair falls forward and covers part of her face from my view. I resist the urge to reach over the table to tuck her hair behind her ears.

She finally looks up at me and smiles mischievously.

"Wanna get out of here?"

I'm already halfway out of my chair before she finishes her sentence, pulling her up by the hand and rushing home.

We haven't had sex as often lately since Emily hasn't been feeling up to it, so I'm taking the chance to help make her feel better to the tune of an orgasm or two.

♥ ♥ ♥ ♥

The neighborhood is quiet, the streetlights already on, as I head back to my apartment after a refreshing hour-long evening run. The competition has ended, and I'm thrilled to have won the cash prize. All those hours of intense training were worth it for the extra money I'll use for my plans.

My breaths are steady as I round the bend. The familiar vehicle parked down the street instantly shatters my composure. While rarer in recent months, its reappearance reminds me of the lingering ghosts of our past.

It's time to shake those ghosts.

My fists tighten, the heat of furious anger radiating through my body. Adrenaline surges through me, a jolt of pure energy that makes my heart pound and sharpen my senses. I am done holding it back.

I have meticulously documented the times that the car parks in front of the house, noting the license plate, make, model, and color. It's normally there by the time I get home from work. The car's been there for an unknown time, and it doesn't belong to any of our neighbors—they all park in their driveways. I dismissed it at first, but the events of Bramblewood Day caused me to reconsider and investigate.

Unlike my usual routine of running past the car, I cross the street and take stock of my surroundings. The street is deserted, and most people are likely finishing dinner now; it's getting late. With Emily resting in our bed, I'm anxious to get back to her.

Approaching the sedan from behind, I slow to a walk, stopping at the driver's side door. The vehicle's tinted windows obscure the identity of its passengers. I rapped impatiently on the windowpane, wanting him to roll it down.

I hear a quiet curse before the window rolls down, which confirms my suspicions.

"Can I help you?" Logan sneers at me.

"Yeah, you can. Explain why you've been parking outside my apartment for weeks."

"What are you talking about? I work for the town."

I give him a cursory once-over. "So, you're currently working? Where's your uniform?"

Logan's face reddens, a fiery mask concealing the fury simmering beneath his skin.

Unconcerned about the potential outcomes, I lean forward and tightly grip the cold metal of his car door, my knuckles turning white with the pressure.

"Listen to me closely. I will not repeat myself." My voice, a barely controlled snarl, grates through clenched teeth as I force out the words. "You're going to leave Emily alone. Leave us alone."

"What are you talking about?" His denial is pathetic.

"I know guys like you. You think no woman could ever move on. But she has. She chose me. Not you," I growl. "You lost her. Now, leave, or I will send all the video surveillance I have of you stalking our apartment when you're off duty to your superior."

I watch gleefully as the color drains from Logan's face. He doesn't need to know it's all a bluff.

"Whatever, man. This isn't what you think it is."

"Sure it's not." My tone is dry, but the contempt is unmistakable.

Stepping back, I glare as he fumbles with his car, glancing back at me before speeding off.

I inhale deeply, my chest expands, and I exhale. Relieved. I hope that's the last I ever have to see or hear from that douche canoe. Emily's been unaware of his persistent surveillance. I assumed Logan had disappeared because she had said nothing about messages from him lately, but he clearly hadn't.

Sending the coward running felt satisfying.

We've finally moved past the haunting memories of our pasts. Emily and I are looking forward to a bright future with our unexpected, but undoubtedly cherished, baby. Our family.

39
Emily

"What about this house?" I send Ben the link to the listing for the house I just found. It's a little out of our budget and about a few towns from where we currently live, but it's a brand new lakefront property. It looks like it's off of a main street. I watch Ben's face as he scrolls through the pictures and looks at the details. He's nodding his head as if he's checking off his requirements in his head.

I know it meets what we're both looking for in a first-time home. I chew on my bottom lip nervously, waiting for his response. We've been casually looking at real estate websites for a house. I'm not too excited about the prospect of moving while being the size of a house, though. Not to mention that I would be essentially useless and can't even help move or lift anything. Plus, we just moved into the apartment less than a year ago, and it's been home to both of us during a challenging time in our lives.

"Let's do a drive-by," Ben finally announces.

"When?"

"Now. Let's go!"

I try to contain my excitement, but when Ben looks up from his phone and gives me a wide grin, I know he is feeling very optimistic about this being the one. We tried to find a nice starter home near our apartment, but none of the listings fit what we were looking for. The ones we found within our budget were much smaller than we needed for a growing family. Either the house was too small and did not have the basic amenities we both wanted, or there was hardly any land. We both agreed having a backyard and space for the baby to run around when they grow up was important.

These qualifications meant we had to widen our search to surrounding towns. We also hired a real estate agent to help us. I texted her the listing so she could help us set up a walk-through.

Ben helps me get up off the couch. A few minutes later, we're in the car and heading to the address listed in a town called Willowbrook. It's only about a twenty-minute commute from our current location. I've never heard of it before, but it looks like a perfect place for a growing family.

When we get closer to the neighborhood, I fidget in my seat with my nose pressed to the window. Despite its proximity to the major highway, the traffic in the area thinned out as we got closer to the center of town. Main Street boasts some mom-and-pop shops, including a bookstore and a coffee shop.

We slowly roll by a small auto shop, and diagonally across the street, we spot the house. The for sale sign makes it easy to recognize, and we pull into the driveway. The house is a colonial with black shutters and a two-car garage. I can see a gleaming lake in the background. The backyard patio extends right up to the water's edge. The home boasts five bedrooms and two and a half bathrooms. The best part is that it's not too far out of our budget to make it happen.

Finally, at the end of Main Street, we turn onto a quiet side street. The quiet streets and well-spaced homes provide privacy. The sidewalks look well-maintained, and I smile at the people who wave at us as we drive through the neighborhood. That checks off the "friendly neighbors" on our list.

I can't believe it's still available. It seems like such a steal. Ben grips my hand, and I look over at him with a big smile. We'll have to come back another time with the real estate agent for a walk-through, but I know this is "the one." Ben kisses my hand and places it on his thigh. He backs out of the driveway, and we drive by the rest of the homes on the street.

I want to pinch myself. This all seems too good to be true. If this is a dream, I hope I never wake up from it. After how the year started, I think I deserve all the good things happening in my life lately.

ꙮ ꙮ ꙮ ꙮ ꙮ

Things moved pretty quickly after we did a walk-through of the house a few days after our drive. I don't know what I expected, but it certainly wasn't us closing on the house a few days before Christmas. We get to pick up our new house keys in a couple of days, and now I have to work on packing what I can handle.

I'm still struggling with pain most days, and it's always worse at night. Despite trying to take things easy, I always push myself a little too much. To be honest, it's not that hard to cross the line between uncomfortable but tolerable to severe pain and needing to lie in bed for the rest of the day. It's frustrating, and I'm so tired of being in pain. I can't even begin to imagine what people who experience chronic pain must feel.

I know there are probably pregnant women who have had worse pregnancies than mine, but it's hard for me to accept that I can't even take the stairs or leave the house without paying for it later. It's like my brain and body are at odds with my capabilities.

In a way, it's a good thing I'm holed up inside the apartment. I've been folding and packing away clothes. It feels like I unpacked my bags just yesterday, but in reality, it has been nearly a year in this apartment.

Ben and I have made many wonderful memories together in such a short time. I never thought my life would look like this a year ago.

It's kind of laughable to think back on the girl I was a year ago. I had my head buried so deep in the sand that I didn't even pay attention to any of the signs that I was unhappy the entire time. I convinced myself that everything was fine and settled for what life had to offer.

Thoughts of Logan flicker across my mind as I continue to pack, but mostly, I'm glad he ended things the way he did. I don't know that Ben and I would have moved in together if he had waited any longer. It feels as if someone had to shake up my life a little in order for all the puzzle pieces to come together.

I wouldn't change anything for the world.

40
Emily

The move to our new home was relatively simple. Our friends were more than happy to help after we bribed them with pizza and beer. Amanda kept me company while Jason and the guys moved all the furniture. We sat in the kitchen and watched her son play on the floor. He's about ready to walk, and every time I look at him, I can't help but think that we'll have one of our own soon. My chest fills with an indescribable warmth I didn't know I was capable of.

I still have a couple of months before what I've started referring to as D-Day, as in delivery day. Having to move into a new home so close to D-Day is not something I would recommend to anyone else. It's been stressful trying to make sure everything was perfect. We already let our landlord know we won't be renewing the lease in February. He's had a few people come by to tour the apartment. I'm not worried he'll have any trouble filling the vacancy.

We found out the gender of the baby a few months ago. It's been hard keeping it a secret, but with the new house and moving, I thought it would be a great opportunity to have a combined housewarming and gender reveal party. Ben and I want to keep the guest list small since we won't have much set up in the house.

My parents said they'd be there, and I'm looking forward to the party.

♥ ♥ ♥ ♥ ♥

I t's been a week since we moved into our new home, and the gender reveal and housewarming party is today. Our parents, siblings, and close friends are in attendance. I'm sitting on the couch, enjoying the feeling of being surrounded by the people that I love. I've been feeling more emotional lately, and I can't blame it solely on pregnancy hormones anymore.

There have been so many things that have happened throughout the past few months that make me feel so thankful for what life has given me. Who knew I needed my heart broken in order to gain so many amazing things?

When it's time to cut the cake, Ben hands me the knife so I can do the honors. I try not to make a mess of the gourmet cake I had custom-made from the same bakery that had made Ben's birthday cake. I know as soon as people see the inside of the cake, they'll know the gender.

I slice a small triangle and pull it out. I plate the cake and turn around to show everyone.

"It's a girl!" someone screams. Everyone starts to cheer and clap, and I hand the knife back to Ben so he can continue cutting slices to serve everyone.

I grab the piece of cake I had and step over to my mom's side. She's been quiet, but I'm glad she came. I offer her the slice, and she hesitantly takes it from my hand.

"It's a girl," she breathes. Tears form in her eyes, and she looks down at the pink layers with white frosting. She accepts the fork and takes a bite of the dessert. I've never been happier to see someone eat cake.

41

Emily

New Year's Eve is fast approaching. While I have so much more to look forward to this year, I've learned to temper my expectations of the date. Am I less superstitious? No, not really, but I've learned that one bad event doesn't make or break your entire year. In fact, there are so many things that can happen in the span of just 365 days.

It feels like it was so much longer than a year ago when Logan had sat me down and broke my heart. At the time, life had looked bleak and scary, but through sheer stubborn will and taking risks, my life has taken a whole different turn.

So, instead of fretting about how I was going to be spending the day, and given my advanced pregnancy and physical limitations, I decided to play it by ear. Ben asked if I wanted to do anything special to mark our first holiday together, and I gave him a non-committal answer. There were many options we could have opted for, and if I hadn't been on bed rest, it would be fun to go out for a nice meal. But, really, all I want to do is stay home and watch the ball drop from the living room of our new house. Ben seems on board with whatever I want to do.

There's always next year, at least.

♥ ♥ ♥ ♥ ♥

"**F**ive-minute warning until the ball drops!" I shout outside at Ben. He disappeared a couple of hours ago to do some work outside. The weather is unseasonably frigid, so I have no idea what he's doing out there.

Ben pops his head out from the side of the house and smiles at me. I eye him suspiciously and go back inside. Waddling back to the couch, I try to get comfortable and prop my feet up, my hands absentmindedly stroking my belly. The baby kicks in response, and I smile. She's most active at night. These days, I feel as big as a house, and everything hurts. I can't wait to welcome our baby girl into the world in a few weeks.

Ben comes inside a few minutes later and says he's going to freshen up. I'm watching the live broadcast of Times Square when he finally comes back downstairs. He's dressed and looking handsome as ever. My eyes roam over his body, drinking in the sight of his sculpted muscles straining against the buttons of his shirt, the fabric stretched taut, revealing the corded strength beneath.

"See something you like?" He smirks, catching me checking him out.

"Oh, definitely," I scoff but smile up at him from my seat.

"Come on. I have to show you something." He gives me a kiss and helps me up off the couch.

"But we'll miss the ball drop!" I know I'm pouting, but I can't help it.

Ben smiles indulgently at me and hands me my coat. He sits me down on the bench and helps me into my winter boots. He leads me outside a few feet before turning around to face me.

"Do you trust me?" he asks, looking deeply into my eyes as he pulls out a scarf from his pocket.

Though I eye the scarf suspiciously, I don't even have to

think about it. I trust him with everything I have. I nod, and he places the scarf over my eyes. The last thing I see is the excited gleam in his eyes. He ties it behind my head and then guides me to where he wants me to go with his hands on my shoulders.

My heart is racing. I have no clue what he's up to. I thought the significance of New Year's Eve would make me feel sad since it was the day that sparked so much change in my life, but I have been excited to have Ben by my side at midnight to ring in the new year. I'm trying not to let a single event define my happiness for the entire year.

He finally stops me and then pushes my shoulders to turn me around. I feel his warmth leave as he steps away from me, the anticipation killing me.

"Okay, you can look."

I whip off the scarf and look around. I'm confused at first. He's set up a string of lights across the pergola in our backyard. In the center is a spinning disco ball. He has his iPad turned on to livestream the Times Square countdown I had just been watching from the couch. The seconds are counting down closer to midnight. Ben also has a projector setup pointing toward the side of the house. The image is of the two of us at a beer fest we went to early in our relationship. "Will you marry me?" is written across the image.

I look around for Ben before I feel a tap on my shoulder. Whirling around, I find Ben on his knee. I gasp and cover my mouth with my hands, tears welling in my eyes. In his hands is a ring box opened up to a beautiful cushion-cut diamond the size of my head.

"Emily Nguyen, the day you asked me to be your roomie was the best day of my life. I want to spend the rest of my life with you and the baby we have made. I love you with every beat of my heart, and I want you to be my wife. Please be my wife and my roomie for life." He gives me a sideways smile.

The sound of the excited crowd escalates as the last ten seconds approach.

10…

"Aren't you supposed to ask me?" I chuckle and give him my hand.

9…

"No, I'm not taking no for an answer." He takes the ring out of the box and slides it on my finger.

8…

He grasps my hand, places a soft kiss on the ring, and stands up to cup my face.

7…

"I love you," I cry into his hands.

6…

"I love you, future wife."

5…

The people continue to count down the seconds to midnight, but I'm not paying any more attention as Ben kisses me hard on the lips, parting them with his tongue, and I moan as our tongues dance. After a few seconds, he pulls away and gives me a big hug.

We sway to the shouts and cheers of people celebrating the new year. Ben holds me tight to his chest and kisses my head as I admire the sparkly new ring.

In the past year, I've learned so much about myself. I've found my self-worth and learned that I don't need to settle for less than what I deserve. I found a man who loves and respects me while giving me the independence I need.

I found love in the countdown.

Most importantly, I found happiness and hope. I have so many things to look forward to, and I can't wait to see what the next year brings.

42

Emily

Charlotte came screaming into the world a few days before her due date at the end of February. She was small for her age but otherwise healthy. She had a full head of dark hair, and her dark grey eyes captured our hearts. We were both elated to welcome her into the world.

Unfortunately, it was not all rainbows and sunshine, as I ended up having postpartum depression or PPD. The chances of me developing PPD were higher, given my health issues during pregnancy. Though I knew it was likely, it was another blow to my self-esteem that I did not bounce back immediately after birth. If anything, it was a struggle to function with a newborn baby who never seemed to sleep through the night, which exacerbated the PPD and subsequent insomnia.

Luckily, Ben's employer had generous paternal leave. He took his part in caring for Charlotte seriously and was vital in maintaining the house. Not only did Charlotte struggle with sleep, but she also had problems with latching, which made breastfeeding a painful and miserable experience for us both. I met with several lactation consultants, and Charlotte eventually figured out how to latch properly. I never realized how happy I would be to see her gain weight by the ounces.

As far as wedding planning goes, it's been on pause until we get our feet back under us again. Now that I'm on medications, my mood has improved, and I'm feeling like myself again. I've started increasing my activity, as the pain has mostly resolved after I gave birth, as expected, though I still feel twinges of pain in my groin. Now that I'm no longer in constant pain, I've been able to enjoy my life a lot more without worrying about the consequences.

Our sex life has taken a hit since Charlotte was born. At first, it was hard for me to feel up to it when I wasn't feeling well. I also felt self-conscious about my postpartum body. Ben has never commented on my weight gain or how I look, and I still feel the heat of his gaze on me when I'm not paying attention. The medications also impacted my libido, which was an unfortunate side effect. More recently, finding time between his work schedule and taking care of Charlotte has been challenging. Since the cost of daycare exceeded my salary, we opted for me to stay home for a while until childcare was more affordable. Things are tight, but we're making it work.

My parents help whenever they can. My mom makes it a habit to stop by each week on her day off to see Charlotte and visit with me. It was awkward initially, but we eventually got into a routine.

One day, when Charlotte was about four months old, my mom was holding Charlotte while I ate the lunch she had made. We were sitting in companionable silence for a few minutes before she cleared her throat.

"I need to apologize to you."

I look at her from across the table, confused by her words.

"For what?"

"I know I was not a good mom to you. I look at Charlotte and think how alike you two are. She is such a joy to be around. I'm sorry for how I treated you." She hugs Charlotte to her chest. "Can you ever forgive me?"

I looked into her tear-filled eyes. She seemed sincere and

distraught by her admission. Emotions surged inside me, and I felt choked up by her unsolicited apology. I fought to keep the tears from falling and nodded. A few hours later, we gave each other a tight hug, and she left. I know it probably took a lot for her to say those words to me, and I am so thankful for them.

I never expected an apology, but hearing the regret in her words lifted a weight off my shoulders.

I put Charlotte to bed in her crib and crawl into Ben's lap. He places his hands on my hips, and we soak in the moment, just enjoying each other. His gaze bores into my soul, to the very center of my being. I've never felt so seen until I look into his hazel eyes.

I cup his face and lift to give him a kiss filled with love and longing. He makes me feel beautiful even on my worst days, and tonight, I want to bathe in the warmth of his affection.

It's not long before he has me pinned underneath him. He quickly undresses me and trails wet kisses down to my center. We don't have a lot of time before Charlotte wakes up again, but he still makes sure that I'm wet and ready to take his cock. Only when I'm writhing and begging does he finally rear up and take his clothes off. He returns to bed, his erect cock in one hand as he strokes himself.

"Hmm. I never tire of looking at you."

He climbs over me and plants a hand near my head. With his other hand, he guides the tip of his cock to my center. After a couple of teasing thrusts, he finally enters me slowly. He lets me get used to him for a few seconds before setting a relentless pace that has me seeing stars.

When he's ready to come, he pulls out of me and gives his cock a few strokes before shooting hot jets of cum on my belly and chest. We have to be careful since I'm not on any birth control. Though we have talked about having another baby, I want to wait a few years before deciding.

The trauma of my pregnancy is still too fresh, and I know I need more time to heal mentally, emotionally, and physically before I can consider carrying another baby. Plus, since Charlotte was unexpected, it would be nice to plan for the next baby instead of having another surprise. That way, I can start treatments like physical therapy and find a therapist to help me through the pregnancy.

epilogue
Emily

FIVE YEARS LATER

Life has been crazy, but I wouldn't have it any other way. We finally got married on the beach in the Bahamas when Charlotte was almost two years old. She was our flower girl, and we were so thrilled to have our little girl walk down the aisle with us. The ceremony was small, with only immediate family and close friends. It was perfect, and I wouldn't have wanted it any other way. We made our vows as the sun set, and it was the most romantic moment of my life since Charlotte arrived.

I started a new job when Charlotte was about three years old. It's at an outpatient clinic and less physically intensive, which I can appreciate as I get older.

It took me a lot longer than a few years to warm up to the idea of being pregnant again. Ben and I talked about having another baby, and when we were both on the same page, I started physical therapy to help prepare my pelvic floor muscles for the added weight. I also found a therapist who could meet with me virtually in case it became difficult to leave the house again.

I felt so much more prepared going into the second pregnancy, and though I was told each pregnancy was different, I was disappointed when I started having symptoms of SPD much sooner this time around. The pain was also much worse, but I could manage working until the third trimester when my doctors had to take me out of work again.

Ben and I welcomed Jackson a few days after his due date in August this past summer. When the PPD hit, we were both prepared for it, and my doctor started me on medications again.

This New Year's Eve is special. We're spending it together as a family. We had our own New Year's Eve party with streamers and party hats. Charlotte helped to decorate and set up the disco ball in our living room. The four of us rang in the New Year early, equipped with last year's countdown in Times Square. When the ball dropped, Charlotte pulled the string connected to the disco ball, letting it drop to the floor in a shiny heap. I scoop up Jackson while Ben gives Charlotte a bear hug. Her excited giggles are music to my ears.

The kids are now in bed, and Ben and I snuggle on the couch with a bottle of pinot noir. The live stream of Times Square plays in the background as the countdown begins. Only this time, I'm lying in the arms of the love of my life, the father of my children, and my best friend and roommate for life.

Despite it all, I would not change a single thing.

Who knew I had to have my heart broken first to get to where I am today?

If this is a dream, I never want to wake up.

THE END

about the author

Lily Anh Nam is an Asian American contemporary romance author. She lives in a quiet New England town with her family and her feline writing companions. Her cats actually typed "the end" to this manuscript because they were tired of being ignored. Though she grew up on a tropical island, her favorite season is fall. Caramel lattes and mint chocolates keep her running.

When not writing, Lily likes to spend time with her family, snuggles with her cats, writing all hours of the day and night, or sleeping. She lives a quiet life as an introvert and has no intention of going into the out without bribery.

You can connect with me on:

https://www.instagram.com/lilyanhnam
www.tiktok.com/@lilyanhnamauthor

www.lilyanhnam.com

acknowledgments

This book has been years in the making. I have wanted to write this story for so long but never had the courage to do so. After a series of misfortune and a healing therapy session with my hairdresser/therapist, I decided to write the damn thing. It has taken many months to get to this point and I could not do it without the love and support of my husband. He graciously took care of the house and kids while I disappeared into the writing cave for hours and hours on end. I am so lucky to be with someone who took my writing dreams seriously.

I want to thank my friends who helped make this possible. If not for Ash answering my millions of questions, I would not have known where to start. I still don't know what I'm doing but she has been so patient with me while I figure out my writing process.

Special thanks to my friend, Tasha, for helping me with branding and typography (among a million other things). I appreciate you more than you know.

I cannot forget to mention my editor, Taylor, who has been so patient as I changed up my manuscript on her a few times before it got to its final version. Working with you was a dream.

Thank you to Lucy for my banners. Your creativity and ingenuity are an inspiration to me.

Special shout out to my friends who kept me sane without realizing it. My alpha reader, Tiffany, who didn't hold back on what I needed to work on. I appreciate your input so much.

My beta readers, you are so appreciated. Jas—your voicenotes were a delight. Thank you for your honesty and making me laugh every day. Miriam—your feedback made me kick my feet in joy. Maria B. for blowing my mind that kitten caboodle is actually "kit and caboodle." Everything I know is a lie.

Thank you to everyone in the group chats that don't exist for your laughter, support, and daily distractions. You kept me sane.

Thanks for reading! Please add a short review on Amazon and let me know what you thought!

Printed in Dunstable, United Kingdom